The ROAD BACK

LIMELIGHT SERIES BOOK #2

PIPER DAVENPORT   JACK DAVENPORT

The Road Back is a work of fiction. Names, characters, places, and incidents are the products of the author's imagination and are used fictitiously. Any resemblance to actual events, locales, or persons, living or dead, is entirely coincidental.

Cover Art
Jackson Jackson

TRIXIE
PUBLISHING

2018 Piper Davenport & Jack Davenport
Copyright © 2018 by Trixie Publishing, Inc.
All rights reserved.

ISBN-13: 978-1548564308
ISBN-10: 1548564303

Published in the United States

All it took was one page and I was immediately hooked on Piper Davenport's writing. Her books contain 100% Alpha and the perfect amount of angst to keep me reading until the wee hours of the morning. I absolutely love each and every one of her fabulous stories. ~ Anna Brooks – Contemporary Romance Author

Get ready to fall head over heels! I fell in love with every single page and spent the last few wishing the book would never end! ~ Harper Sloan, NY Times & USA Today Bestselling Author

Piper Davenport just reached deep into my heart and gave me every warm and fuzzy possible. ~ Geri Glenn, Author of the Kings of Korruption MC Series

To the countless drummers that helped shape my life.
Thank you for showing me who real musicians are.

Special shout out to our favorite mother-flicker, Cyndi.
We love you, Beanie!

Jack

One year ago…

MUCH LIKE DANTE'S Inferno, my vision of hell contains many circles. I currently found myself in two of them simultaneously…sitting inside a corporate coffee hut…in an airport. The demons were disguised as bleary-eyed commuters and the smell of burned coffee beans replaced the traditional sulfuric stench of brimstone, but it was hell nonetheless. In my former life, at four in the morning, Rex Haddon and I would've been sitting in a very dark bar, many empties between us, after having closed the place down. Times had certainly changed.

"Why now?" I asked.

"What do you mean?" Rex challenged. "Why *not* now?"

"Well, for starters, last time I checked, rock was dead."

"You're lucky nineteen-year-old Jack Henry isn't around to hear you say that." Rex grinned. He wasn't wrong. Nineteen-year-old Jack Henry was a scrappy, angry young man who took his music very seriously.

I ignored him and continued, "What I mean, is rock music is far from thriving right now. Everyone is listening to Katy Lovato and Selena Grande Latte."

"Melody Morgan," Rex corrected.

"What?" I asked flatly.

"You didn't raise a teenage daughter. They listen to Melody Morgan."

"What-the-fuck-ever," I breathed out. "That's my point exactly. It's all mouse ear music these days. Who'd even care about a RatHound reunion?"

"First of all, rock is far from dead, my friend," Rex countered. "It's only dead if we let it die...your words. Plus, there are plenty of great young rock bands that are hungry and raw; like we were. Bands like, Rival Sons, Arms Race Radio, and Roses for Anna."

"Man, you know I don't listen to the radio or watch those TV music game shows."

"I'm not talking about TV star shit; I'm talking about real bands playing real music. It's time, Jack." Rex looked at me more seriously now. "It's time for us to start making music again. It's time for you to start playing again and remind the people what real music sounds like."

I took a swig of coffee. I had to admit, it was an interesting proposition. It had been ten years since the band had called it quits. Technically, we never officially broke up; we all just went our separate ways and never played together again. Perhaps it was a small distinction to our fans, but it was a big one to us. Unlike a lot of bands back then, we never hated each other or had a big falling out. We destroyed ourselves from within, one at a time. "It's just a summer tour, Jack." Rex paused for effect. "On the west coast."

"And an E.P.," I added.

"Yes, the label would like us to record a three song E.P. to promote the tour."

"Rex, I haven't touched a pair of sticks in years and you want me to go into the studio and then straight out on the road for six weeks?"

"I have faith in you. I know the animal drummer is still in there. You just have to let him out."

"Ladies and gentlemen, I'd like to invite all first-class passengers for flight 2137 to Spain to begin boarding at this time."

"That's my flight," I said, and quickly stood up. "I'll think about it."

"Hold on, that's it? I haven't seen you in years, you can only meet me at the ass crack of dawn in the airport, and now you're off to Spain? What gives, man?" Rex rose to his feet. "Are we still friends or what?"

"Of course we are." I exhaled deeply. "I'm just not sure about the timing. I have a lot of things coming up, you know how it is."

"Yeah, I know very well 'how it is,' that's why I'm here, trying to intercept you before you're off to your next adventure kite surfing in Bali, kick boxing in Thailand, or scaling the ice caves of Freeze-your-balls-offistan, or whatever it is this month.

"Rex, I'm going to Spain to relax and take photos. I promise I'll think about it and get back to you as soon as I can."

"As soon as you can? What does that mean? Do they not have cell towers in Spain? Shit, man, send me a smoke signal or a homing pigeon, just let me know *soon!* I have an opening band in mind, and am in negotiations with someone to manage the tour."

I smiled. "I promise I'll get back to you, just give me a little time to think about it and don't get your hopes up."

Jack

Present day...

I PULLED UP to the studio and parked the truck. I still wasn't sure this was a good idea, or if I was up to the task, but I'd said yes and that was that. I'm not entirely sure why I'd agreed to a reunion tour, but I suppose I had run out of excuses, not to mention, it was always hard for me to say no to Rex. As the youngest member of the band, I'd always looked up to him and he'd never steered me wrong. Not to say that Rex wasn't without his faults, he *was* a lead singer, after all.

"Jack Henry Gornitzka, as I live and breathe," Robbie said as he came bounding out to greet me.

"Mitchell Roberts, the third," I yelled back, before embracing my old friend. "Robbie" as he was known, was the band's guitarist, and the one most responsible for my joining RatHound.

"How was Spain?" he asked.

"It was great. I got a lot of great shots. Hopefully some of them will make it into the next book." I shook my head and grinned. "But forget about all that, what are *you* up to? How are Lisa and the twins?"

"They're about to go into college. Can you believe that? Shit man, I still remember sneaking your scrawny ass into the clubs, and now I've got kids in college!"

I'd been a big fan of the band back when they were still playing clubs up and down the Pacific Northwest. I never missed a show when they played in Portland, and often drove as far as Tacoma and Seattle to see them. I was four or five years younger than anyone in the band, but I knew all their songs, inside and out, and was obsessed with their original drummer, Ben Gorman. Ben was kicked out for being drunk all the time. Ironic, since the rest of the guys were too, the only difference being they could still do their job shit-faced. Ben couldn't. He'd been my hero, but that still didn't mean I didn't jump at the chance to audition when Robbie asked.

"I wasn't sure you'd have the balls to show up." Robbie grinned from ear to ear. "You know all our songs?" These were the same words he spoke to me the night that I'd auditioned back in 1990. I was just a scrawny kid trying not to embarrass myself in front of my local heroes, but I was prepared, played my ass off, and ultimately got the gig.

"C'mon, we're just getting set up," he said, and led me into the studio.

Fastback Studios would be our home for the next three weeks or so. We used to rehearse here back in the day, then Rex had bought the property, even though he'd built a state-of-the-art studio on the back of his guest house. He said he "wanted to pay it forward" for other young musicians and gave them the best deal in town.

For now, however, we'd be using the space to rehearse for the tour and to record a few new songs. Pacific Records, our old label, was paying for the studio time in hopes to woo us back to them. I wasn't convinced that we'd be able to make any kind of waves in today's ever-changing music business, but was intrigued by the idea of creating new music with Rex and Robbie.

Rex was sitting at the mixing board, along with a recording engineer. He stood up as we entered and reached out to hug me. "It's great to see you, brother. I can't believe we're all finally here."

"I'm having a hard time wrapping my mind around the whole thing, to be honest with you," I admitted.

"Well, you'd better get used to it fast, we've got a shit ton of songs to run through and we can't play them without our drummer."

It was good to see Rex so happy. He'd been through a lot (hell, *I'd* put him through a lot), and he and Roxie had literally saved my life after Pam died.

"Roxie is so excited to have you back home. Your room is ready and waiting as usual."

Rex and Roxie had a guest house that had served as my home for two years. They took care of me when my world fell apart, and I owed them my life. They were the most generous people I had ever known and I learned a lot about being in the service of others from them.

Rex was a spiritual man, with an almost Shaman-like presence. Many great singers from Jim Morrison to Bono had this kind of vibe and it made them very attractive to people. I had been drawn to him as a kid and I still found myself in awe of him at times.

"I can't believe she keeps that place empty for me. You

guys should use that space and I can stay in a hotel."

"Use the 'Jack Henry Suite' for something else? Like what? Plus, what would we do with your drums?" He smiled. "Although, I must admit we did have another drummer staying there not too long ago."

"Is this Lucy's guy?" I asked flatly.

"His name is Bam and he's her husband Jack," he responded.

"How the hell could you let her marry a drummer, Rex? What the fuck were you thinking?"

Rex smiled even wider. "What can I say, Uncle Jack? She loves him."

I crossed my arms. "Don't much care about that fleeting emotion, Rex. I'm worried about her being with a musician, a drummer no less."

"You're so cruel to your own kind Jack, you always have been."

"Damn right. I hate drummers!"

Rex laughed. "Well, rest assured, Bam's one of the good ones."

"Guys or drummers?" I asked.

"Both, actually. I think you'll be impressed with Roses for Anna's music and Bam's playing."

"I'm not easily impressed."

"I'm aware," he said. "But, you should know, he's a *big* fan of yours, buddy."

"Shit. Are you kidding me?"

"Nope." He grinned. "He's not supposed to know that I know that."

"Well, young marriages can be annulled, and if worse comes to worse, drummers and their bodies can easily disappear while on tour."

"Don't worry brother, I've already fitted him for his own road case in case he ever hurts Lucy." Rex laughed and showed me around the studio complex.

"This place looks a lot less run-down than even five years ago," I said, surveying my surroundings. Last time I'd visited Rex and Roxie, Rex had brought me here to listen to a couple of the bands rehearsing. I loved being in recording studios. They were like sacred ground to me.

"Yeah. We did a big upgrade two years ago. Hired a new engineer."

"You're shittin' me."

"Yeah, dumbass, I'm shittin' you." Rex grinned. "Vic isn't goin' anywhere."

Vic Masters had been our engineer since almost the beginning of the band. He was an extension of us, another member, if you will, and I didn't think I'd ever trust my drum tones to anyone else. Our producers might have changed from project to project, but Vic was always the engineer.

Vic looked up briefly, smiled, nodded, then went right back to his work. I noticed my drums had already been set up and it sparked a feeling inside me I hadn't felt in a long time. Until very recently, I hadn't played in years. I'd started rehearsing on my own a few weeks ago, and the blisters and sore muscles were proof.

Drums are a very demanding instrument, and time spent away from the drum kit is much like ignoring the gym. Getting back into drumming shape is slow and painful, and the fact that I was now approaching my mid-forties, certainly didn't help.

Vic had set my drum kit up in the center of the tracking room and had already begun setting up microphones.

"Wow, looks like we're already set up to record." I was both excited and nervous about this. "I didn't know we'd be diving right in."

"Don't worry about the mics. Just ignore them. I figured we may as well record our rehearsals so we can go back and review the "game tape" as a band." Rex smiled reassuringly. "You're not the only one that hasn't played some of these songs in years."

"Yeah, but you've played a lot of them with your little merry band of imposters," I challenged with a grin.

"Oh, so we're going to dive right in, Jackie?" He laughed. "Someone had to fly the RatHound flag while you were out hanging from a cliff face somewhere. Plus, the guys in my band don't grumble as much as you two old ladies."

"Fair enough," I relented. "How are Teddy and Spike? I hope they're not pissed about being out of a job this summer."

"They're great and they are excited for us, actually. They send their best and will be at the opening show."

"No pressure," I said. "I can just imagine going out and shitting the bed in front of my replacement."

"Pressure? You're Jack fucking Henry!" he joked. "Modern Drummer magazine's 1991 Newcomer of the Year. This should be a cakewalk for you, unless magazines can't be trusted."

"Well, obviously magazines can't be trusted. People named you Sexiest Man Alive...twice!"

It was good to be with my brothers-in-arms again. I can't truly explain the bond that bandmates share. It exists somewhere between brotherhood and war buddies. Musicians share an intimacy that few people can ever understand, but, on the other hand, we're selfish and often times, guarded. Taking the piss out of one another was the best way to keep each other on the same, level playing field.

"Screw both you guys!" Robbie chimed in. "The only magazine that ever wanted me on a cover was MAD."

Laughter filled the air for the next half an hour, as we eased ourselves into the task at hand. I'd made the final tweaks on my drum kit and we were tuned up and ready to play.

"No time like the present, gents. Shall we?" Rex said into his mic.

"Whatta you want to start with, Jack?" Robbie asked.

"I feel pretty solid on 'Pages.' How about that?"

The guys nodded, and for the first time in as long as I can remember, I counted my band in.

* * *

Hadley

I was *late*. Crap! I was supposed to meet Lucy Nelson at the RatHound rehearsal ten minutes ago, but I'd gotten lost. Stupid Seattle. It was too big. I was a southern girl unused to the big city...although, truth be told, I got lost in Mobile as well.

I pulled my rental car up to the front of Fastback Studios where the band had been rehearsing for several weeks, and took a deep breath. I was about to walk onto holy ground and I wasn't quite sure how to react. RatHound was one of the biggest bands on the planet, and they were heading out on tour with Roses for Anna (the band I now managed), which meant more pressure than I think I was prepared for.

I slid out of my car, grabbed my purse and portfolio (I was still old school enough to write everything down on paper), and walked inside.

The receptionist smiled and I made my way to her desk. "Hi. I'm Hadley Simon. I'm meeting Lucy Nelson for the RatHound rehearsal."

"They've been expecting you," she said, and rose to her feet, handing me a visitor badge. "I'll walk you back."

"Thank you," I said as I stuck my badge on my blouse, and followed her to a back studio area. I stepped inside and froze. I couldn't have moved if I'd wanted to. I was alone in a small reception area; one large glass window gave me a direct line of sight to the mixing room, another looked into the tracking room…and the drummer.

I couldn't breathe. He drummed like a man possessed. His long, dark hair fell over his full beard as he hit the skins, but then he looked up, and piercing blue eyes that caught mine as I stood transfixed, stared into my soul. I swallowed convulsively and then forced a slight smile. To so many musicians and music fans around the world, Jack Henry was a god. I had just become one of his willing worshipers.

He stared at me for a few tense seconds and then grinned over at Rex Haddon, and I lost my connection to him. I scurried through another door which led me to the mixing room where Lucy hugged me as soon as I walked inside. "You made it."

I nodded. "I'm so sorry I'm late. I got a little turned around."

Lucy Nelson, nee Haddon, as she was newly married to Bam Nelson, the Roses for Anna drummer, was a full-figured, drop-dead gorgeous red-head whose father had put her in charge of this tour, and his band. Even though I was several years older than her, and had been doing my job for a while now, I knew I'd be able to learn a lot from her. We were both newly appointed female managers in the male-dominated music industry, and we were very thankful to have each other's support on our maiden tour. We'd become very close in a short period of time, as Bam was one of my dearest friends.

"Don't worry about it; it's easy to get lost in this city." She grinned. "Next time, I'll have Sully pick you up."

Sully was Lucy's driver, and rather gorgeous himself. He looked a lot like Pierce Brosnan, only he smiled a hell of a lot less. I guess that was part of his job, though, as he also served as her personal security detail.

"Where's Bam?" I asked. "I thought he'd be here."

Lucy nodded. "He's making a coffee run."

I raised an eyebrow. *"He's* making a coffee run? Don't they have studio runners here?"

"Normally yes, but this is a pretty 'closed set,' so-to-speak, plus he doesn't much mind."

"You've got him trained that quickly? What's your secret?"

"He's learning that if I'm happy during the day, he's extra happy at night."

"Lucy Nelson, are you exchanging caffeinated beverages for sexual favors?"

"Absolutely," she said. "I like my lattes like I like my men, strong, bold, and slightly whipped."

I couldn't stop a giggle…just as the door to the tracking room opened and Rex walked in. "Hey, Vic, can we get the playback? Oh, hey, Hadley."

"Hey, Rex, how are you?"

He leaned down and kissed my cheek. "I'm good. How 'bout you?"

"Haven't had coffee yet, so ask me again in ten minutes." I walked over to the pot sitting in the corner and forced myself not to shudder at the powdered creamer. I needed caffeine ASAP or I'd rage like…well, like a non-caffeinated Hadley Simon.

He chuckled. "You got it."

My eyes couldn't stop glancing over his shoulder just in case Mr. Sex on a Stick walked in. I didn't have to wait long. Robbie, their guitarist pushed through the door, followed by Jack.

I squared my shoulders and forced myself to look away from my own personal Dionysus. It was all I could do to stop myself from dropping to my knees as he pulled his hair into a messy man bun.

Twelve years ago, when his wife died of cancer, Jack Henry went off the grid and all but vanished from public life. I was twenty-three at the time and getting ready to start my senior year in college. I was certainly very familiar with RatHound and their music, but admittedly was never much of a fan. I was a country girl, so I mostly listened to country music. In fact, Roses for Anna was the first rock band I'd worked with. Jack had been considered a sex symbol due to his boyish good looks, he'd never really pinged my radar, because, one, he was a rocker, and two, he was the clean-cut boyish type and I'd always been a sucker for dark and rugged men.

Today, the creature who stood in front of me was *all* man and my girl parts were pinging *and* ponging.

"Hadley, have you met Jack and Robbie?" Lucy asked.

"No," I managed to squeak out.

Robbie shook my hand, gave me a quick nod, and then focused back on engineer Vic, but Jack…Jack took my hand and held it a little longer than I expected while he gave me a slow, sexy smile and said, "Hi Hadley. It's nice to meet you."

Ping!

Jack

HOLY SHIT, IT felt good to play again. After my wife's death, I'd spent the better part of the past decade at the bottom of a bottle, and almost died twice myself. My life now consisted of travel, photography, and little else. This kept me sober and sane, but completely disconnected from those I loved. For the longest time, it was simply too painful to be around anyone or anything that reminded me of Pam; this included my band and my drums. Being back behind my drum kit, playing with my best friends, was an amazing feeling. I hadn't truly realized how much I'd missed this and was surprised with how quickly we were gelling as a band.

"Let's play it again," I said to my fellow bandmates.

Rex chuckled. "You certainly seem to be back in fighting form."

"Getting there," I replied. "It was a lot easier when we were kids, that's for damn sure."

"It was a lot easier with cocaine too," Robbie joked.

"Everything was certainly faster." We all laughed before launching into the song one more time.

I attacked the kit with everything I had. Playing the drums is a constant dance between tension and release, and there is an art behind hitting hard but not destroying your body in the process. Even though I was in shape and very physically active, I was still trying to find that line. After a few weeks of practice, I felt far more prepared for the tour than I thought I'd be, and we'd managed to write and record some great new tunes. As the song came to an end, we looked at each other knowingly. Seasoned musicians know when they've nailed a take.

"Shit, my brothers! Now *that* was great!" Robbie said. "Let's go listen to that one."

I took off my headphones, grabbed a towel and headed for the control room. Rex entered first, followed by Robbie and me. As I entered I spotted Lucy, Rex's daughter and our new manager. Months ago, Rex mentioned he'd been inter-viewing a new manager, but you could have knocked me over with a feather when I found out it was little Lucy. She was like a niece to me and Pam, and I adored her. She had always been a sweet but feisty kid, and had blossomed into an independent kick-ass woman. In the short weeks that I'd been able to see her work, I was convinced she was more than capable to handle the job. Her husband had yet to make an appearance at Fastback, however, and every time I men-tioned him to Lucy, or asked any questions, she'd simply smile and say, "I can't wait for you to meet him."

Before I could greet Lucy, she introduced me to the other woman in the room. I hadn't noticed her at first, but stopped breathing the moment I saw her. "Hadley, have you met Jack and Robbie?" Lucy asked the gorgeous brunette.

Robbie shook her hand first while my brain raced for something charming to say.

"Hi, Hadley. It's nice to meet you," was all I could manage, but it made little difference either way. She barely looked at me.

"Nice to meet you, too," she replied in a quiet, southern accented voice. Then she cracked only the smallest of smiles and broke eye contact with me as quickly as possible.

"Hadley is Roses for Anna's manager," Lucy continued. "She's also a good friend, so you boys better be on your best behavior around her." She raised an eyebrow and wagged a finger at us.

"When have we ever been anything less than absolute gentlemen?" Robbie asked playfully.

"You forget I'm your manager now and therefore have access to your permanent record, old man," Lucy replied. "Hadley and I have some transportation matters to iron out today for the tour, but I wanted her to meet you all first."

I heard every word Lucy was saying, but realized I had been staring at Hadley the entire time. She was unbelievably beautiful, with shoulder length dark brown hair and an amazing body. Curvy and soft in all the right places. Her ice blue eyes were framed by thick black glasses, completing her sexy librarian look. She appeared to be somewhat detached, but not cold. I tried again to engage her.

"How long have you been with Roses for Anna?"

"A few years," she answered, quickly adding, "But, I've only been their manager for a few months."

"Sounds like there were some *issues* with the previous

manager," I said. A large sum of money had gone missing and a federal investigation led to the arrest of Roses for Anna's former manager.

She smiled again briefly and once again turned away, focusing her attention back to Lucy. "We should probably get started."

"Oh, okay, sure. We can go over everything in the lounge. Let me just grab my laptop." Lucy turned her attention back to the band for a moment. "You guys sound amazing, by the way. The new songs are incredible."

"Thanks Lucy," I said before making eye contact with Hadley again. "It was really nice meeting you. I guess we'll being seeing you around."

She nodded and slipped through the door to the lounge. I looked at Lucy and shrugged. I assumed that Hadley had guys in the business hitting on her all the time and probably figured I was going to pounce on her like the others.

This couldn't be further from the truth. I hadn't had any kind of meaningful relationship with a woman since Pam, and hadn't even dated over the past two years. Meaningless hookups and nights spent in drunken oblivion were well behind me and I wasn't about to do anything to jeopardize my sobriety or sanity.

Still, there was something about this woman that drew me to her. She clearly showed no interest in me, but it made little difference. Her lack of eye contact didn't negate the fact that I was obviously going to be very distracted with Hadley hanging around the studio.

* * *

Hadley

Well, holy crap on a stick! I licked my lips. That man was dangerous. *God bless America!* He stared into my soul like he could read my mind.

A gentle hand tapped my knee. "Hadley?"

"Hmm?" I glanced at Lucy who sat across from me.

"You okay?"

"Oh, yes." I smiled. "Sorry. We were talking about bus companies."

Lucy raised an eyebrow, but just as she opened her mouth to speak, Bam walked in carrying several coffees. She set her laptop aside and rose to her feet. "Perfect timing."

Bam leaned down to kiss her quickly. "You miss me?"

She took the coffee with her name on it and took a swig. "Hmm-mmm, yep, it was you I missed," she crooned and stroked the paper cup.

Bam chuckled and handed me a Frap. "Thanks, Bam. You read my mind."

"One of my super powers." He grinned. "Plus, I know what you're like before coffee."

"I'd object to you speaking to me like you know me, but I love you for getting me coffee, so you're forgiven...for now."

"You ready to meet Jack today?" Lucy asked.

"Absolutely not," Bam said.

I could relate to his nervousness, even if he wasn't nervous for the same reasons I had been. I saw motion in the window and Jack smiled at me as he sat back behind his drums. I smiled back, pushing my glasses back up my nose and focusing back on Bam. "Looks like they're getting back to it."

"See Luce, it looks like they're busy. I can meet him tomorrow," Bam said.

"Why don't you hang with us?" I suggested. "You can weigh in on a few things."

"I should really get going, but maybe I'll stop by later," he said.

"Okay sure," I said only half paying attention to Bam's

words. I could *not* stop looking at the man behind the glass.

"Earth to Hadley," Bam said.

"Sorry." I shook my head and faced him. "I don't know what's wrong with me today...I'm so distracted."

"I wonder why," Lucy retorted, giving me a cheeky grin.

I could feel the heat flood my face, so I dropped my head, letting my hair fall around it as I pretended to check my notes. Clearing my throat, I said, "So, I think we should go with—"

"Hey, Dad," Lucy said, interrupting me. "Sorry, Hadley. Give us a second, okay?"

"No problem." I looked up and smiled at Rex who'd just walked in from the sound booth. Jack was right behind him and I squirmed in my seat.

Damn it, I needed a little relief.

I had a feeling I was going to be imagining a certain long-haired man while I was utilizing my B.O.B. later.

Jack smiled, his eyes lingering on me for a few precious seconds. I felt like I might internally combust if I didn't look away, so I pretended to read over my notes.

Bam said nothing, but winked at me, using this distraction as an opportunity to slip out of the room unnoticed. It was funny to see him so nervous to meet his hero. Apparently being nervous around Jack Henry is a thing around here.

It was times like this that I fantasized about being a different person. The kind of person, for example, that would have a meaningless sexual fling with a rock star. I wasn't Lucy and he wasn't Bam, so I wasn't about to entertain some sort of romantic fantasy, but I wondered what it would be like to simply have a tryst with Jack Henry. Sure, he was older, probably had a harem of women, and we were in business together...but who cares? I could be one of those women that could ignore all that for what I was sure would be mind blowing sex—right?

Fat chance. I was a good girl and I knew it. Besides, I'd heard what happened to the band manager before Lucy and squashed that thought. According to Lucy, she'd gotten the job because the previous woman had cornered Rex and tried to remove his clothing. She was promptly fired and Lucy took over.

I had no intention of losing my job. I had plans. Ones that didn't include dallying with a member of RatHound. Regardless of how sexy the man was, damn it.

"Hey."

I jumped.

"Sorry," Jack said. "I didn't mean to scare you."

Ohmigod, his voice. It did things to me. Naughty things.

I rose to my feet and set my notepad on the chair. I needed to be taller...I felt too vulnerable sitting. "No, you didn't. I was in the zone, I guess."

We were alone and I was immediately struck dumb with the closeness of the man, plus...more pinging. *So much pinging.*

Lucy had left me a few minutes ago, heading in to join Bam.

"I was just finishing up. Are you guys still rehearsing?"

Jack shook his head. "Everyone's listening to the play-back."

"Shouldn't you be in there?"

"I'm good right here, Hadley."

I bit my lip. I tried to slide my hand into my pocket but overshot the mark, and I couldn't figure out who the hell sewed the damn thing shut. If I tried to move my hands to my back pockets, I was painfully aware that my double-D's would be thrust out and make me look like a B-52 bomber coming in for a landing.

I didn't want to cross my arms because that shows you're closed...which, to him, I wasn't.

Shit! I didn't know what to do with my hands.

"You want to come listen with us?" Jack offered.

"Um, sure. Yes, that would be great."

* * *

Jack

Hadley and I stood shoulder-to-shoulder against the back wall of the studio. The new song we were working on pumped through the monitors, and my bandmates were all smiles. Even though Rex had a successful solo career, and Robbie had stayed very active as a session and touring bassist for several bands over the years, there was simply no denying the magic that happened when the three of us played together. There's no hiding in a trio. Each player has to be one hundred percent committed at all times. It's an exciting and dangerous way to make music that requires a level of intimacy and telepathy between players.

I leaned over to Hadley, still facing the monitors. "What do you think?"

She smiled. "It really sounds great. You guys sound like... like...*you*."

"Well I guess that's better than sounding like Bieber," I said dryly.

She turned to me quickly her hand shooting up to her mouth. "Oh, no, I just meant that you guys sound just as good as you did back—"

"Back when we were young? Back when we toured via brontosaurus?"

"*No*, I just meant—"

I smiled wide to let her off the hook and she playfully smacked my arm. "You're mean," she said.

My entire body stiffened in reaction to her touch. Hadley was beautiful, so I wasn't surprised at my physical attraction to her, but I felt there was something more to her

22

and I wanted to know what it was.

"Didn't your mother ever tell you to stay away from musicians?"

"Yes, that's why I like them so much," she said.

"Oh, you like musicians, do you?"

"Well, yes, I mean, that's why I work for them...um, *with* them."

"I get it." I smiled. I could swear she was blushing, and for the first time I absolutely *wanted* her. "Seriously, though. Why *do* you want to spend your life hanging around musicians? You look smarter than that."

"Thanks, I guess." She giggled. "I never really thought about it, I've just always loved music and wanted to be a part of it somehow."

"Why not pick up an instrument or sing, or start a band?"

"I did," she said smiling. "I mean I do."

"What, have a band?"

"I did, before I got into the management side. I was the singer in a group, but I started out as a drummer."

At that moment, I was dead sure of one thing; there was no way in hell I was going to be able to stay away from this woman.

"A chick drummer?" I asked smiling ear to ear.

"Excuse me? I am not a chick!" I couldn't tell if Hadley was mocking offence or not, but was ready to defend my case.

"I didn't say you were a chick. I would never do so, to you or any other woman," I said flatly.

"But you—"

I interrupted her protest. "I said you were a 'chick drummer.'"

Hadley turned to face me and blinked slowly from behind her thick black frames. I began to get hard, and straightened my posture to help conceal the bulge in my pants. She was unbelievably sexy. It was hard to believe this was the same woman that wouldn't make eye contact with me two weeks ago. I was beginning to see there were many layers to Hadley Simon.

"How is calling me a chick drummer any different than calling me a chick?"

"It just is," I said, refusing to be the first to break eye contact.

"It just is? That's not an answer. You can't just add "drummer" to the end of something and claim that in negates the previous word."

"I agree. That would be absurd."

She tightened her face into what I assumed was meant to be a scowl but came across as the sexiest pout I'd ever seen.

"Explain," she said.

"Look, it's very simple. A chick is an outdated diet-misogynistic term used by roadies in the 70s who smelled like van carpet and bong water."

Hadley's face cracked a very small smile.

"Chick drummers, on the other hand are powerful, beautiful, thunder goddesses that possess the ability to shake the very foundations of earth."

"Is that all?" she asked, choking back laughter.

"Actually, no, they're also the sexiest of all creation."

I smiled slowly and she swallowed...fuckin' sexy as hell.

Hadley

OH, MY WORD. I needed to get a handle on my attraction to this man. "You're insane."

"Doesn't mean I'm wrong," he countered.

He leaned just a little closer and I swallowed convulsively.

"Jack!" Rex called. "Ready?"

"Yep," he said, still staring at me. "We'll continue this conversation later. I have several questions for you, Hadley Simon."

He grinned and pushed away from the wall. I slipped out of the room unnoticed and used this break in the action to hightail it back to the hotel. Lucy and I were done for the day, and since I had a few things to do from my side, I chose to do it out of the presence of the sexy as hell Jack Henry.

I let myself into my current home away from home and flopped onto the bed for a few minutes of emotional TLC before forcing myself to open my laptop.

* * *

The next morning, I arrived at the studio before everyone. I had just checked out of my hotel and picked up keys from Bam and Lucy, as I would be watching their home (and their dog) for the next week while they headed home to pack the band up and be back in Seattle before the first show in three weeks.

I saw light in the mixing room, so peeked my head in and saw Vic already setting up. "Hi, Vic."

"Hey, Hadley. How are you?"

"I'm good. I'm going to make a much-needed coffee run, what can I get you?"

"Coffee black and a bagel would be great."

I smiled. "I can do that."

I stepped back into the lounging area and jotted down Vic's order just as Rex walked in, Jack and Robbie following.

My heartbeat sped up a little when Jack gave me a sexy smile. "Hey, Hadley."

"Hi," I breathed out, then cleared my throat and tried to speak without sounding like a sex starved school girl. "Um, I'm going to make a coffee run. What can I get you guys?"

"I'll come with you," Jack offered.

"You will?" Rex challenged.

I didn't hear his answer as I dropped my head to rummage in my purse for my keys.

"I'll drive," Jack said.

"Oh, it's okay. I'm sure you have a lot to do. I'm happy to go."

He smiled again. "I'm driving, Hadley."

Glancing around the room, I found us alone and I really had no reason to argue, especially since I'd appreciate the help, so I nodded.

"Ready?"

I nodded again and we walked out to the parking lot where he ushered me into his gigantic pick-up. No joke, I had to climb it to get inside.

"You good?" he asked once I was in the passenger seat.

"I think that qualifies as a workout," I retorted, and he chuckled as he closed me in.

"Sorry. Sometimes my photography takes me off the beaten path enough to need this monster."

He climbed up beside me and we headed to Flick's Beanery, Jack's favorite local coffee shop. He helped me down and we walked up to the counter to order. I gave the young girl behind the counter my name and order but barley saw signs of life register on her face. I was surprised when Jack ordered a chai tea and I said as much while we waited.

"I'd imagined you ordering something a bit stronger," I said.

"I've had my first cup of rocket fuel this morning, so should probably ease off a little."

"That leaves room for a bit of a sugar rush then, doesn't it?" I gestured towards the display counter filled with pastries.

"My body's a temple," he explained. "I try to eat as healthy as possible."

"Yeah, well, my body's a temple, too, but I'm working on an addition."

Jack dropped his head back and laughed, causing me to blush when a few people looked our way. "Damn, you're funny."

I smiled. "Am I?"

He knocked his shoulder gently against mine. "Very."

"Thank you."

"You and Lucy workin' on more tour plans today?"

"Lucy and Bam left this morning."

"Right...they're prepping the band. I thought that was tomorrow."

"Nope, they left this morning."

"Sully flyin'?"

I nodded and then sighed. "Private jet. Such a glamorous life."

A shadow crossed his face. "Trust me, there's a price to pay, and few are able to pay without it costing them everything."

"Sorry," I whispered.

"Don't be. It's all good."

I bit my lip and forced myself not to pry. Admittedly, I was kind of a nosy nelly, but only if I cared about the person. Jack was quickly becoming that for me, and I needed to shut it down before I became too attached to him. Our relationship was that of a short-termed business nature, and although I enjoyed his company, I had to remind myself not to get distracted. We waited for what seemed like forever for our order as the line stacked up behind us. I was starting to feel the effects of this so-far caffeine free morning, and my mood would not be improved by the sloth-like pace of the shop's only barista on shift.

"Henley," the blue-haired girl behind the counter called out in what I could only assume was the voice that took the least amount of energy. "Henley," she repeated again to no one's response. "Henley," she said a third time now in an annoyed tone and looking directly at me.

"Oh, me? Hadley. I'm Hadley."

"The order says Henley, it's written on the cups," the

barista said flatly.

"I'm sure it is," I responded. "Is it a large black coffee, a medium latte, a Chai and two bagels?"

"Uh huh."

"Okay then that's my order and I'm Hadley," I said smiling, happy to finally clear up any remaining confusion once and for all.

"The cups say Henley," she said.

I stood silent, in pure un-caffeinated disbelief for at least five full seconds before finally asking, "Who took my order?"

"I did."

"Right, and who took my name?"

"Me."

"Great, now who's in charge of writing the name of the customer down on the cups?"

"I am," she said proudly, cracking her first and only smile of the exchange.

"Super, so do you think it's more likely that I don't know my own name, or that you simply didn't dedicate enough of your limited attention span to learning my name and correctly writing it down?"

"Well…"

I awaited her response as if awaiting an answer to an earnest prayer.

She held one of the cups up. "The order says Henley."

I turned to look at Jack who was standing three feet behind me choking back laughter. He was clearly not going to offer me any assistance and seemed to be enjoying himself immensely.

I leaned down to look at her nametag which read *Tabitha*.

"Look Tabitha," I started.

"It's pronounced ta-bee-tha," she said, now using her snotty tone again.

"I'm sorry, what the fresh hell did you just say?"

"My name's not Tabitha, it's Tabeetha," she repeated.

"No, that can't be right, because your name is spelled like Tabitha, which is a completely normal, *real* name," I corrected. "Your name has an 'I' in it, not two Es, making it Tab-I-tha. You can't just go making up new pronunciations of perfectly normal names and expect society to just go along with it! So, just because your parents were confused about how names work, and then passed that down to you, doesn't mean *I'm* confused about *my* name." I stood inches away from her face, my hands now clutching the cardboard tray containing 'Henley's' order.

Tabeetha paused for a moment, and then burst into tears.

"I—" Was all I could manage to get out before she ran off to the back of the shop. I wasn't sure what or who was behind the swinging double doors she'd just disappeared through, but I didn't care much to find out.

Jack stepped up to the counter, quickly pulled a fifty-dollar bill from his wallet, and threw it on the counter. He grabbed our drinks, then my hand, and high-tailed us out of the coffee shop.

"Well, I guess we won't be going to Flicks any more for coffee," he said with a laugh as we climbed back into "Bone Crusher" and sped out of the parking lot.

I let out a frustrated squeak, partly because I was mad at myself for making another woman cry, and partly because I was still irritated at said woman for making me *make* her cry.

"You okay?"

"Yes," I said with a sigh. "At least we got the coffee."

"Forget the coffee," he said. "Nothing in the world will wake you up better than roughing up a nineteen-year-old barista."

"You could have helped," I snapped.

"You seemed like you had her on the ropes all by yourself there, champ. There was no need to tag me in."

I huffed. "Now I'm going to have to go back and apologize."

"Wow, doesn't take you long to snap back to your good girl southern self, huh?"

"Mediocrity drives me to a level that I should probably get a handle on."

"Or, maybe people need to learn to do better."

I rubbed my temples. "It's not her fault she's a product of a society that just doesn't give a shit."

He chuckled. "Okay, Hadley. Give yourself a break, huh? She'll get over it."

I nodded and stared out the window. Jack turned on the radio and 'Pour Some Sugar on Me' came blaring through the truck's cabin.

"Now we're talking! A soundtrack is now rolling to our little Bonnie and Clyde story. A little Def Leppard!"

I laughed. "There's no way you like this music."

"What are you talking about? I love Def Leppard," he said with a straight face.

"What? I thought all you grunge guys were supposed to hate hair metal," I challenged.

"First of all," he said, turning down the music. "We weren't a 'grunge' band, whatever that means, and 'hair metal' was an equally horrible name to pin on musicians. A ton of us suburban rocker kids cut our teeth on Motley Crüe, Van Halen, and Whitesnake. Sure, it all got silly and over the top, and us and bands like us were more than happy to help usher in new sounds, but we respected those guys for what they did."

"Wow, I never would have thought," I said smiling.

"How do *you* know this song?

"My mom loved it and played it around the house when my daddy wasn't around, so I grew up loving it."

"Your dad not a big Leppard fan?"

"No, he wasn't a big fan of 'fun of any kind,' unless it involved Jesus or judging people. I suppose his favorite kinds of activities involved both."

"Ah, one of *those* guys."

"No, he *was* the guy they based those guys on. Remember the dad in Footloose? That guy was laid back compared to my daddy, I'm not joking."

"Wow. How the heck did you go from no Rock and Roll in the house to hitting the road with us filthy animals?"

"I started out singing and playing piano, or whatever else needed to be done at the church we went to. My father was an elder in the church and so our whole family was expected to serve the church, and serve we did. But it always bothered me that I wasn't allowed to play drums…because I was a lady."

"Well, now we have something else in common," he said.

"You were a lady who couldn't play drums?"

He chuckled. "I didn't grow up religious or anything, but I did go to church youth group as a kid and that's where I discovered the drums."

"You're kidding?"

"Nope. Totally serious. I was twelve years old and my best friend dragged me there with the promise of lots of cute girls."

"Were there a lot of cute girls?"

"A couple, but that didn't matter once the band started."

"That good, huh?"

"Oh, god no, they were horrible. They were all guys in their forties with skullets."

"Skullets?" I laughed.

"Yeah, you know. Mullett in the back, balding on top. Anyway, they were basically playing bad classic rock with a lot of Jesus thrown in, but the minute I heard those drums I was transfixed. I'd never been that close to a full set of drums being played and I knew right then and there I had to play them myself. The drummer was really cool and he let me try them out after youth group was over."

"Did you ask your parents for a drum set that Christmas?"

"No way. At that time things were pretty tense in my house, and even if we had the money, there was no way it was going toward a drum set for me. My parents were fighting all the time and on the verge of divorcing, so I hung around the church and those drums as often as I could. Eventually, they asked me to start playing in the youth band and from then I was off and running."

"Drumming for the Lord, huh?"

"Amen sister!" He smiled. "But then when I was sixteen, my parents divorced and my mom moved us from sunny California to rainy Portland."

"No more church?" I asked

"Not so much. More like more drumming, more chasing girls, a lot of smoking pot and a hell of a lot of being generally pissed off at the world. Typical child of divorce stuff, I guess. Who cares about that? What about you? How did you end up playing the drums?"

"The church secretary was a sweet lady that had a soft spot for me. She'd let me into the sanctuary when I knew my father wasn't around."

"He'd really have a problem if he knew you were playing the drums?"

"A problem? No. More like, he'd disown me."

"No way," he said in disbelief.

"We barely speak now because he disapproves of my 'choice of occupation.'"

"Wow, I guess he missed all those parts in the Bible about love, forgiveness, peace and grace."

"You don't know the half of it. My mother, on the other hand, was a little more tolerable, at least on the music front.

She gave me her old CDs and I'd get behind the church drums and play along to all these great 80's bands in my earbuds."

"That sounds adorable." Jack grinned from ear-to-ear, which was some sort of wake-up call to the butterflies in my stomach.

I continued, "The older I got, the more I sang in church and my father eventually started to really push me into a career as a Christian country singer, or as he called it a 'ministry.' I did as I was told and hated every minute of it."

"Why do it then?"

"To make my daddy happy. To make God happy. To make people who heard me sing happy."

"Everybody but you," he deduced.

"Something like that, yes." I glanced out the window again. "Now I don't really speak to either of my parents and I can't seem to find the energy to give even one shit about it." I shook my head. "I can't believe I'm telling you this."

"Why not?"

"Because it's not really like me. I don't share."

"I like you sharing," he said as he pulled into the studio parking lot.

"Well, we're back." I smiled and pushed open the door.

"Hold up. Don't want you to fall out."

I rolled my eyes, but waited for him to climb out and walk to my side of the truck. He lifted me down, then grabbed the coffees, and I followed him inside.

My heart reeled with emotions I'd never really experienced, which was quickly followed up with my brain reminding me I was here to do a job and flirting with a man more than a decade older than me was not part of said job.

Gah! I needed to slow this down.

I spent the rest of the day making sure our interaction was friendly, but highly professional, and I snuck out when they went back in to rehearse their final song of the day. I had all the notes I needed for Roses for Anna, and the band had my number should they need something Lucy couldn't handle from Alabama.

I slipped into Bam and Lucy's apartment, grabbed their toy poodle, Mammoth, and took him out for a walk. I decided that since their apartment was so close to a couple of good restaurants, I'd order food and take it back to eat while I worked.

It gave me some time to get my head together...even if my heart still objected.

CHAPTER FOUR

Jack

THREE DAYS LATER, my recent levity had gone to shit with the realization that we were rapidly approaching a "No Groove Tuesday." That's what we'd dubbed rehearsal nights where we just couldn't seem to make the magic happen. In the early days of the band, should an official N.G.T. be declared, we'd go out for tacos and beer rather than spend further energy beating a dead horse. Some nights, try as you might, you just can't put things together musically.

I stopped playing the song we were currently slogging through and the band came to a halt. "Are we playing it too slow? It feels slow."

"It feels like shit is what it feels like," Robbie said.

"I've been playing it at one hundred and twenty-seven beats per minute with my band," Rex added.

Rex had gone on to a successful solo career after the disintegration of RatHound, which of course meant he'd been playing a large selection of our back catalogue in his live shows. His band was really good, but lacked the raw power that RatHound was known for. His solo act was a bit 'slick' for my taste, with a slightly higher emphasis on production, which meant his band would play to a 'click track' for each song, which is simply a metronome that is fed into each player's in-ear monitors. Although common practice for most bands these days, I hated it.

"I'm not playing to a fucking click, Rex."

"I never said I wanted you to. Ease up man, just trying to help," Rex retorted, sounding slightly hurt.

"Sorry, brother. Everything just feels like shit today. My sticks feel heavy and I'm just not finding the pocket."

"That's it! Taco time," Robbie said, taking his guitar off. He placed his signature '72 Telecaster Deluxe on the nearest stand and declared, "Gentlemen, I officially call our first no groove Tuesday. Can I get a second?"

"Indeed," I said.

"So fucking be it!" Rex yelled.

It was a little on the early side of the day for dinner, but I wasn't going to be the one to break tradition. Plus, we weren't far from Rocco's Tacos, and despite its name and northwest location, served amazing Mexican food. We grabbed our jackets and headed out. As we crossed through the lobby, Hadley came in through the front door.

"Hey there," she said smiling, a cardboard coffee cup in each hand, pushing the door open with her glorious ass. "Since I now know you like chai, I grabbed you one from Flick's since I was there apologizing to Tabitha and her manager."

It had been a few days since Hadley had been around the studio. I'd love to say I hadn't really noticed, but I had. What's more, her absence may have been adding to my increasing shit mood.

"Oh, wow, thanks. We're just heading out for dinner," I replied, trying not to sound too happy to see her.

"Dinner? It's barely past three o' clock. Are y'all headed to Denny's for the early bird special?"

"Ouch. She comes baring caffeinated gifts and then sneaks in a cheap shot about my age."

Hadley gasped and turned bright red. "Ohmigod, I didn't mean that as a...I just meant...because it's so early..."

I smiled wide to let her off the hook, but I couldn't help but admit I loved watching her squirm a little. Seeing her flustered did something to me.

"We're actually headed to Rocco's to lick our musical wounds."

"Rough day at the office, huh?" she deduced.

"A no groove Tuesday has been called which only tacos and cheap Mexican beer can solve. Since we're all sober guys, we're left to depend on the goodness of the world's most perfect food. Hopefully it'll be enough to get us through this."

"No groove Tuesday? But it's Friday."

"Not anymore," I said in defeat.

"Jackie Boy, you comin'?" Robbie called out.

"I should get going, thanks again for the chai, it'll go great with my fish tacos." I raised my cup to her.

"Maybe I'll see you later if I'm still here," she said, and I hoped this would be the case.

* * *

The smell inside Rocco's was what I imagined heaven to smell like. One thing I don't hear many addicts talk about is how much more food means to you once drugs, alcohol, and cigarettes are out of the picture.

I inhaled deeply and groaned. "God, I've missed this place."

We instinctively headed for our normal corner booth which was currently unoccupied and took this rare quiet moment to get caught up. It felt good to get away from the music side of our relationship, and hear about their families and how well they were doing. On the other hand, being back in Seattle, around all these familiar faces and places, was stirring up the ghosts of my past. My thoughts turned to Pam with increasing frequency and my obvious attraction to Hadley was not helping matters.

"Earth to Jack." Robbie snapped his finger, bringing my full attention back to the table.

"Sorry, guys. I'm somewhere else today I guess."

"What's up?" Rex asked. "Anything we can do?"

"You talk to your sponsor?" Robbie asked.

"Last night, I'm good there. I'm just in a shit mood. I guess I'm tired. I dunno." I knew it was more than that. I could feel the familiar dark clouds coming in, and was acutely aware of how quickly this could turn into a storm. I think it's pretty safe to assume most artists suffer from some form of depression and I was no exception, but I didn't want to bring the mood down. Besides, there wasn't a damn thing they could do about it

"Hearing about your families, being back in town, playing all these old songs. I guess it all makes me miss Pam a little more."

Rex and Robbie leaned in, a look of concern on their faces.

"No, no, no. I'm okay," I said in an attempt to diffuse any pity party that may be thrown. "It's okay that I miss her. It's okay for me to be sad. I've had to learn how to process these feelings, it's just a lot to take in right now."

Secretly my thoughts turned to Hadley once more. I could *not* shake the feeling that she could somehow make me feel better. Over the years, I had learned to trust my feelings, but be wary of making decisions based on them. Hadley made me want to do foolish things. I simply couldn't shake her. I was clearly attracted to her, but keeping my sexual appetite in check was a part of my recovery, not to mention the colossally bad idea of hooking up with the opening band's manager.

"I'm good guys. I'm finding my sea legs again and it's going to take a little time. You've both had some time to figure out how to tour sober and this is new territory for me. Shit this *all* feels new to me."

"We get it, and we're in this together," Rex said in typical big brother fashion. "Speaking of together"—He and Robbie glanced at each other—"you and Hadley?" he asked raising an eyebrow.

"No," I answered flatly.

"Okay, alright," he said raising his hands in surrender. "Just thought I'd ask, you may want to be careful, because I think she's got a crush on a certain drummer."

"Thanks, Dad," I snapped back, perhaps a little harder than intended. "I'm not going to do anything stupid."

"Just don't forget that I *know* you Jackie Boy," he said in his typical loving, but slightly pointed fashion. Rex's words had weight, and if he laid them on you, you felt it.

"I'm good," I said more reassuringly than deserved.

"Alright, now if we're done taping today's episode of the View, how about we get some tacos in us pronto." Robbie—the ever-present voice of reason.

* * *

When we got back to the studio, I was happy to see Hadley was still there, but Rex's words still hung over me like a dark cloud. I knew he was right, and if I wasn't careful, I was going to end up hurting Hadley, or worse yet, I'd end up fucking her and then we'd both be in trouble.

Hadley was in her normal spot at the lobby coffee table, with her laptop and her circa 1993 day-planner, looking as dead sexy as usual. I had to make peace with the fact that, although I enjoyed looking at the lovely Miss Simon, I had to abandon all thoughts of touching. My flirtations needed to come to an immediate end.

"How was Taco Tuesday?" she asked looking up from her laptop.

"No groove Tuesday," I corrected her, and tried not to laugh. She was undeniably gorgeous, but I reminded myself that my feelings were purely physical. For both our sakes, I needed to avoid engaging any further.

"Oh, right," she smiled and giggled. "I still say you were sneaking out for the Moons Over My Hammy," she teased.

I had to slow this train down and took her playful crack as an opportunity to apply the brakes. "Because were old. Still funny," I deadpanned.

Hadley shifted in her seat and her usually flushed cheeks fell to a chalky pallor. "Oh. I…" She looked down. "Well, I hope the rest of your day is more productive," she said softly in a way that made me want to jump off the nearest bridge.

"Me too." I smiled slightly in an attempt to ease up a bit, but Hadley avoided eye contact. I was clearly going to have to figure out how to regulate around this woman. From my current position, I could see Lucy and Rex through the control room window.

"Lucy's back from Montgomery?" I asked Hadley, in an effort to change the subject.

"Yes, she's in there with Bam," she said, her tone brightening a bit. "I think Lucy wanted to introduce you two."

Shit, this is all I need tonight, to entertain the hound dog that didn't have the sense to do what I'm doing now; avoid getting involved with women in the business.

"Oh, cool," I said, but felt my tone was likely less than convincing.

"He's a great guy and a big fan," Hadley said coolly.

"So I've heard."

We stared at each other but said nothing.

"Alright, I'll catch you later," I said trying to awkwardly dismount from this horrible conversation, and pushed through the studio doors.

* * *

Hadley

I took a deep breath and sent Bam some good thoughts... Jack Henry was his hero and this was the first time he was meeting him. I couldn't imagine what I'd do if I met one of mine...particularly with the warning of, "Never meet your heroes" floating out there.

Jack seemed more than a little *off* tonight. He was on edge and distant but admittedly I barely knew him and I could have been imagining things. Either way, I was sure they'd have a ton in common and just hoped Bam wasn't too nervous.

I took a few minutes of alone time to push aside my hurt. I shouldn't be hurt. I didn't know him. But I liked him. This man. The one who confused me, and I tried to analyze why. I didn't like men who confused me. I liked men who were straight-forward, ones who liked me *just* a little more than I liked them, and who didn't press me into sex.

I'd had three sexual partners and they'd been when I'd finally gotten away from the oppression of my church, and on the road with musicians, so I'd only been having sex for the last five years or so. I liked it. It was fun. It wasn't mind-blowing, but I was okay with that. I'd had orgasms...

not every time, but sometimes, and I was always in an exclusive relationship, no cheating, no drama. Just nice, easy, and fun. Until it was time to be over and then the splits were amicable. I was still friends with all of them. There was no back biting, revenge porn, nasty messages on social media. Just lovers who had decided to go their separate ways. Easy peasy.

But Jack? God, Jack confused the hell out of me. He made me laugh, made my heart race, made my lady parts ping. My lady parts had never pinged…at least not like this. I spent most of my day wondering what Jack would taste like as I fantasized licking his entire body.

I shook off my pornographic notions and went back to the schedule.

Jack

'D HEARD ROSES for Anna's music by now and Rex wasn't wrong, the guys could play. Despite their more obvious southern rock leanings, I could hear a younger version of RatHound woven into their music. I could also hear a half dozen of our peers like Pearl Jam and Soundgarden that I'm sure had influenced them. I could respect what Roses for Anna was doing, but honestly had a hard time listening to them objectively. The truth was, I didn't want to like them. At least, I didn't want to like their drummer, who was currently walking toward me with a goofy grin on his face.

"Jack this is Bam Nelson, my son-in-law and drummer

for Roses for Anna," Rex said as he ushered Bam toward me.

"It's an honor to meet you, sir. I'm a huge fan. Really, you have no idea," Bam said as we shook hands. "I've been listening to you since I was a kid."

Shit, I'm getting old.

"Call me Jack, please."

"Okay...please call me Bam...but, why wouldn't you?" he said nervously, still shaking my hand. "That's my name, well my real name is Beau, but you wouldn't know that—"

"Sorry, Uncle Jack, Bam is a big fan," Lucy said smiling, gently pulling her husband's hand from mine.

Little Lucy has a husband. Shit, I really am getting old.

Lucy was more than just Rex's daughter to me. She was the daughter Pam and I never had. We were about her age when we got married which made me miss Pam all over again.

"Uncle Jack, are you okay?" Lucy asked, and snapped me back to the present.

"What? Oh, I'm sorry. It's nice to meet you Bam. Rex says you're a good guy and that you understand you'll be murdered without haste if you hurt our little girl here."

"Yes sir, um...Jack, I've been informed," he replied with a grin. I did have to admit that despite his awe shucks charm, he did seem genuine. I also had to admit that Lucy was far from stupid, so if she saw something in this...*drummer*, perhaps I should be open minded. On the other hand, I hated the idea of Lucy rushing into a marriage with any Tom, Dick, or Ringo.

I choked back my urge to cast him out of the inner sanctum. "Lucy said you'd be okay with hanging around and watching us work out some new songs," I said.

"Okay with it?" Bam grinned. "Yeah, I'd love that, as long as I'm not in y'all's way."

"I'm sure you know your way around a studio and know

how not to be in the way," I said dryly.

"Don't worry, Uncle Jack, he can sit right here next to me on the couch," Lucy said.

"Watch it, little lady. Shouldn't the two of you have a Bible between you at all times?"

"Not any more. Remember, we're married now, Uncle Jack," Lucy said, proudly displaying her ring adorned finger.

"Oh, right. Does that matter?"

"Now you're sounding like the God-fearin' people of Elwood, Alabama," Bam said.

"Never been there, but I guess you could say I grew up playing in the church, nonetheless."

"No shit?"

"No shit."

I cracked a smile at the pair and excused myself back to the tracking room where I joined Rex and Robbie.

The space had high, vaulted ceilings that suited the kind of big, open drum sounds we liked on our recordings. The room was separated from the control room by two thick panes of soundproof glass. A pushbutton talkback mic and wall-mount speaker system was used to communicate between the two rooms.

"He's a good kid, right?" Rex asked while putting his bass on.

"How the hell should I know, Rex? I met the guy for two minutes. You're the one that seems so in love with him," I snapped.

"Jeez, lighten up Francis, I was just asking what you thought of my new son-in-law," he replied.

"Guys," Robbie said.

"I already told you what I thought, Rex," I snapped back. "I asked you what the fuck you were thinking letting her marry a drummer."

"Hey, guys," Robbie said, this time a little more impatiently.

"Hold on a second, Robbie," Rex said, and turned back to me. "I didn't *let* Lucy do anything. She's an adult and she made her own decision."

"Bullshit, Rex! If you had told her you thought it was a bad idea she would have listened to you. She respects your opinion."

"Yes, she does, and in my opinion, I think Bam is a good man. Not to mention, I trust my daughter's judgment. What the fuck is your problem?"

"He's a musician, Rex! He's clearly a road dog and he's going to hurt her. He'll be a piece of shit like every other guy we know out there, and she'll get her heart broken."

"Guys!" Robbie yelled one final time.

Rex and I snapped our heads toward him in unison and shouted. "What, Robbie?"

"Vic wanted me to remind you that the talkback mic to the control room is currently broken...and stuck in the on position."

We turned around and looked through the glass to see Lucy and Bam sitting stone-faced on the sofa. Lucy wasn't stone-faced for long. She dissolved into a puddle of tears and Bam shot me a look that could kill.

Fuck!

I set my sticks down and rose to my feet just as Hadley wrapped an arm around Lucy and headed toward the exit.

Bam stormed into the room, his hands fisted at his side. "What the fuck, asshole?"

"Hey man, I'm sorry, don't take it personally, I—"

"Don't take it personally?" Bam cut me off and pressed forward. "Are you fucking kidding me? Did you see the look on Lucy's face?"

"You weren't supposed to hear any of that. It was meant to be a private conversation," I argued.

"Right. A conversation with two other people about *me*

and *my wife*," he snapped.

The expression on Bam's face grew more intense. I relaxed my posture and took a step back. Bam was right to protect Lucy and he was right to get in my face. I was being a prick about the whole thing, but it still didn't change the way I felt or my opinion on the subject. I didn't want Lucy to settle for a musician who would end up destroying her life.

"Lucy is family to me," I said, adjusting my tone. "She was family to my wife. I'm very protective of her."

"No shit. So is everyone else in her life. Hell, I practically had to kung-fu fight her driver/assassin, Rex just about roasted me on his gigantic fire pit..."

I glanced at Rex who simply grinned and nodded.

Bam continued, "The fact that y'all feel she needs protecting is the funniest part. She can handle herself just fine."

"That's just it, Bam. You don't know what she can or cannot handle because you don't know what's out there. You weren't around back in the day. There's a big reason Rex had to hire Sully, and Robbie had to hire someone for his twins. There are a lot of shady people out there and the bigger you get, the crazier they get."

"Well, she has me to protect her now, so you can all back the fuck off," he said in a slow, low tone.

"Bam, with all due respect, I don't know you," I replied.

"Respect? You think you've been treating me with respect? Was that respectful to Lucy? To speak about her like she's a child, or her father's property? What about all your shitty assumptions about my commitment to her, or my intentions? You're right, you don't fucking know me, so what gives you the right to judge me?"

I could clearly see Bam's anger level was entering the red zone and he didn't appear like a man you'd want to mess with when pushed too far. I was well schooled in several forms of martial arts, but this guy looked like he was a little more schooled in 'broken beer bottle to the neck,' and I didn't care to push my luck.

"You're right," I replied.

Before I could get another word out, Bam said, "Excuse me, I have to go find Lucy," and left the room.

Robbie grinned. "I believe that young pup just gave you a tongue lashing, Jack."

"Fuck you, Robbie."

Rex walked up to me and laid his hand on my shoulder. "Still question his devotion to Lucy?" he asked softly.

"I'm starting to see what you mean."

* * *

Hadley

After Bam had walked into the bathroom and taken over the comforting Lucy position, I stepped back into the studio waiting area and focused on my notepad again. I jotted down a few things I needed to look at when I got back to Rex and Roxie's, which is where I'd do the most work...I needed complete quiet which this environment didn't offer. Roxie had insisted I stay with them once Bam and Lucy returned, which meant I'd be heading over there tonight after practice. I really liked Roxie and couldn't wait to get to know the woman who'd raised Lucy.

There was a lot to do when planning a tour, but Lucy and I had most of it covered, and since Lucy had a relationship with every manager at every venue where we'd be performing, our planning had been a hell of a lot smoother than previous ones.

Although, I think part of the reason things were going so well, was because Roses for Anna had finally fired Chas Chambers, their previous manager and the man who'd stolen a great deal of their money. I had managed to get some of it back, but I couldn't get it all, and I still had pangs of guilt surrounding that fact.

Bam had assured me everything was okay and he didn't care about the rest of the money, but I still wished I'd discovered Chas's evilness sooner. I sighed.

"You okay?"

I jumped a little and glanced up at Jack.

"Sorry," he said with a gentle smile. "Didn't mean to scare you...again."

I rose to my feet and squared my shoulders. "I'm good."

"Can you tell me which way Lucy went?"

"I can..."

"Okay, which way?"

"Oh, I'm not going to."

He crossed his arms. "Why not?"

I matched his stance. If the jerk was going to close himself off to me, I would close myself off to him. "Maybe because she's upset and you're the reason why. Or maybe because you said some pretty nasty things about one of my favorite people. Take your pick."

He dropped his head back and stared at the ceiling for several seconds before meeting my eyes again. "Not that it's any of your business, but I plan to apologize."

Rude!

"Well, that's good. I hope you plan to apologize to Bam as well, because let me tell you something about my best friend. Bam Nelson's had a tough life, but you'd *never* know it. He's always happy, always sweet, and will *always* stand up for the 'little guy.' He's the best person I've ever known and you saying all those nasty things about him makes me angry. So angry, I might just lose my religion."

"Had—"

"I'm not done," I snapped.

His eyes widened and he got a weird (but sexy, damn it) look on his face. I jabbed a finger toward the door. "That man...the one you called a piece of shit—"

"I never called him a piece of shit."

"You implied it," I countered.

He took a couple of deep breaths, but didn't argue. "That man is more than my best friend, he's my brother. And like any big sister, I will cut anyone who steps to him. And if you're that little bitch, don't doubt that I will cut you too."

A familiar chuckle had me turning my head toward the sound.

"You can put your sword away, Had," Bam said.

Lucy stood slightly behind Bam, her hand on his arm.

I uncrossed my arms and stepped away from Jack. I watched his body war with his emotions...it was written all over his face as he studied Bam and Lucy.

"Lucy, honey, will you let me apologize?" he asked.

"Go for it," she said, her eyes still wet.

"I was a jerk. I won't make excuses, but I let my love for you overtake my common sense. I never had the honor of raisin' my own daughter, so you were it, baby girl, and I overreacted. Will you forgive me?"

Lucy rushed to him, wrapping her arms around his waist. "I love you, Uncle Jack. Of course I'll forgive you." She glanced up at him. "But if you *ever* disrespect my husband again, I will kick you in the family jewels."

Jack chuckled, giving her a gentle squeeze. "I'll keep that in mind."

"Jack?" Rex called as he opened the door. "We need to get back to it."

Jack called back. "I'll be right there, I'm doing something more important." He cupped Lucy's face. "I really am sorry, honey."

"I appreciate that, Uncle Jack."

He kissed her forehead and turned to Bam. He extended his hand and said "I owe you and your bride an apology. I was in the wrong, and for what it's worth, I respect you for standing up for Lucy. I hope you can accept my apology and my hand in friendship. I'm usually a great guy...you can ask the two friends I have."

Bam chuckled, along with the room and shook Jack's hand.

"Shit, man, if I'd know you were such a dick I wouldn't have dropped all that coin on your signature drumsticks for all those years."

Jack erupted into laughter and it was great to see the dark cloud that had been hanging over him all day finally lift.

"Thanks, man, and again I'm sorry everyone. I guess all of *this* has been a little rougher on me than I thought." He smiled and gave a genuine bow of humility to all in the room before exiting to the tracking room.

"Ohmigod, I was *not* expecting that," Lucy said with a sigh, sitting back on the sofa. "Jack's always been the quiet one. He never says boo to anyone, let alone shares his feelings like that."

Bam shook his head. "He's hurting, obviously. Just gotta be patient."

I rolled my eyes. "Well, he better think twice about doing that again."

"He will," Lucy assured me. "Despite what you just saw, he's a really good man, so he tends to learn from his mistakes."

I gave her a wary smile. I envied Lucy in a lot of ways. She had a great family and seemed to forgive easily. Plus, she married Bam. Don't get me wrong, I wasn't romantically interested in Bam, but I *would* like to meet and fall in love with someone as good as him. Unfortunately, I didn't trust people enough to let myself get that close. Too much betrayal.

"Alright, I'm gonna head out," Bam said, kissing Lucy's temple.

"Okay, honey. We're almost done here, so I'll be home in a bit."

He nodded and walked out, and Lucy and I got back to work.

Hadley

LUCY'S DRIVER, SULLY, pulled the car to a stop outside of the palatial mansion on the water that was Lucy's childhood home. It looked like something from a Tuscan village, not a Seattle suburb. Good lord, it was magnificent.

"Welcome, Miss Simon," Sully said after he opened my door.

"I'm not sure this is a good idea."

He smiled. "If Mrs. Haddon invites you to stay, you don't have much of a choice, so I'd highly suggest you just go with it."

I took a deep breath and climbed out of the car.

"I'll take care of your bags," Sully said.

"Oh, thank you." I also knew offering to help wasn't really an option, so I went with that as well and let him take care of it.

"Hadley," Roxie cried as she pulled open the front door. "Welcome!"

"Hi, Roxie. Thank you so much for having me."

"It's our pleasure, honey." She pulled me in for a hug and smiled. "We love company. Let me show you to your room, then I'll give you a tour of the house."

I nodded and followed her up the right side of the foyer (they had a freakin' double staircase for Pete's sake), and down the hall in the middle of the upper landing.

Roxie opened the third door on the left and stood back so I could precede her inside. My mouth dropped open of its own accord and I let out a quiet, "Wow."

The room was bigger than my apartment at home. A slight over exaggeration, but not much of one. A king-sized bed sat between two large windows that overlooked the water, and a door to the right led to a large bathroom with a to-die-for claw-foot tub.

"I figured you might like the room with the tub," Roxie said. "I love mine."

"You read my mind," I confirmed.

She chuckled. "Sully will leave your bags. Do you want to freshen up before dinner?"

"No, I'm good," I said. "Can I help?"

"Sure," she said. "I'll show you around."

I dropped my purse beside one of the dressers and followed Roxie downstairs. She took me through all of the rooms downstairs and I was sure I'd need a map to find my way around. We ended in the kitchen and I heard male voices as we approached.

Walking inside, I stalled.

Jack turned after grabbing a bottled water from the refrigerator and an expression that I'm sure matched mine appeared on his face. "Hadley. What are you doin' here?"

"I...," I stuttered.

"She's staying with us until you go on tour," Roxie said. "Isn't that great, Jack?"

He nodded, but his face belied his agreement.

"Rex. Got a minute?" Jack asked, and walked out of the room.

I shook off his cold reaction to me and forced a smile. "Okay, what can I do?"

Roxie pulled out the makings of a salad and dropped it on the counter. "How do you feel about leafy greens?"

"I love leafy greens," I said, and went about doing my best culinary work.

* * *

Jack

Rex followed me into the game room and closed the door behind us. "What's up?"

"What the fuck, man?" I snapped.

"What the fuck, what?"

I scowled. "Why is Hadley here, Rex?"

"Roxie invited her to stay...well, we invited her to stay. It seemed pointless for her to pay for a hotel when she was doin' stuff for us as well. She and Lucy have become good friends and they're workin' well together, so she asked if Hadley could stay. You know Rox, she loves hostin—"

"Rex," I growled.

"You said you didn't have a thing for her."

"I *don't*!"

"Seems like the gentleman doth protest too much, Jackie boy."

"I think thou should fucketh the fuck off, Rex."

Rex grinned.

"Let's just say I don't have a thing for her, and I'm trying to keep it that way."

"Well shit, that's gonna be a little harder with her stayin' here, isn't it?" Rex mused while dragging his hands through his hair.

"Ya think?"

Rex shrugged. "Brother, you said there was nothing between you, and besides, it wouldn't have mattered anyway once Roxie had made up her mind to have her stay here."

Rex and I snapped our attention to one another and in unison said, "Roxie!"

"She can't know about any of this," I said frantically. I couldn't actually think of which scenario was more frightening, Roxie trying to keep us apart, or trying to play matchmaker.

"No kidding," Rex replied. "If she finds out, she'll meddle, and no good could come from that. What the hell is it with you drummers and managers anyway?"

"Are you really judging me? You're the one that keeps introducing all of us!"

"Keep your voice down, Roxie will hear us," Rex shushed.

I continued my rant, now whispering, "You just about arranged Lucy and Bam's marriage. Did he have to pay you in drum skins and cowbells?"

"No, actual animal pelts and cows."

I scowled. "Explain to me why you'd parade a smoking hot young, amazing woman in front of me, and then blame me for noticing. A woman that seems absolutely perfect in every way imaginable and *I'm* the asshole for getting a little hung up."

"Just so I'm clear," Rex said grinning. "You *don't* have a thing for her."

"I did ask you to kindly fucketh off, didn't I?"

"The salads are ready!" Roxie called. "What are you boys doing in there?"

Rex replied. "Nothing, just talking about..." he froze and glanced at me, apparently momentarily unable to think of a suitable cover story.

"The tour," I said, just as he came to and simultaneously blurted out, "cars!"

"Cars on the tour," I said

"Tour transportation!" we yelled triumphantly in unison.

"Well, come eat, you can talk about whatever it is you're not really talking about later," she responded.

* * *

Hadley

I slinked away to bed as soon as I possibly could. Dinner had been an exercise of trying to ignore the closeness of one Jack Henry, the gorgeous, but increasingly hostile man I'd been forced to sit next to.

I was currently lying in a quickly cooling tub and nursing my hurt feelings. Good lord, the tour hadn't even started, and I already needed it to be over. I needed to go home and hole up in my little apartment in Mobile where I could hide for a while.

I reluctantly pulled the plug and climbed out of the tub, wishing I had a glass (or a bottle) of wine. Roxie didn't keep any alcohol in her house, which made sense, but I would have really liked a little right about now.

I pulled on undies and a T-shirt, brushed out my hair and then decided to see if I could find some ice cream or something to get my sugar fix. I glanced at the big fluffy robe Roxie gave me hanging on the back of the door, but decided to forgo it, and headed downstairs.

Opening the freezer, I'd hit pay dirt. I grabbed one of six individual mint-chocolate-chip ice cream containers (thank God someone in the house has a sweet tooth), a spoon, and headed back upstairs when I heard a thump and a familiar voice exclaim, "Shit!" I froze in place and squeezed my eyes closed. There I stood, half-naked, foraging for ice cream and Jack Henry was in the house... somewhere. "Jack?" I called out as quietly as possible. "Is that you?" the last thing I needed was to wake up the whole house. It took a minute, but then he said, "Yeah, Hadley, it's me."

I looked around for something to cover myself, but only found a tea towel draped over the oven door handle. "Are you hiding?" I called out, still scrambling for anything to provide me with a shred of modesty.

"Kind of, yeah."

He appeared before me as though he were an apparition and I froze in place, the pathetically undersized tea towel, barely covering my thighs. God, he was gorgeous. He wore a pair of black PJ pants, slung low on his hips and a long-sleeved ribbed Henley that left nothing to the imagination in regard to his lean but extremely cut body.

"Fuck," Jack breathed out. "Uh, I'm sorry, I didn't know you were, ah..."

"Why are you here?" I blurted out.

"I live here when I'm home."

"I mean, here, Jack. In the kitchen. Shouldn't you be out at the guest house?"

He gave me a smile that made me want to drop my towel. "Roxie keeps a stash of tea that helps me sleep."

"Oh, okay. Can you, um, turn around or, close your eyes or something, so I can just scoot past you." I felt the heat rising to my face.

"Sure, but I'd rather have your company. Here, you can wear these," he said before swiftly removing his pajama bottoms, tossing them to me before I could protest.

He now stood before me in his grey boxer-briefs, giving me a great look at his bulge. Not that you could miss it. I tried to compose myself and slipped on his pants. He smelled amazing and his intoxicating scent was driving me crazy.

"You can't sleep, huh?" I asked, trying to hide the fact that I was becoming increasingly hot and bothered.

"Not so much. I'm not much of a sleeper anyway, but I've got a lot on my mind."

I wrinkled my nose. "I'm sorry. Thinking about the tour?"

He leaned against the counter and crossed his arms. "Among other things."

"Like what," I asked.

"Not what, who," he said smiling, now slowly circling to my side of the kitchen island.

He studied me and then suddenly, his lips were on mine. I gasped in surprise, which gave him better access to my mouth, then his tongue touched mine and I was done.

I slid my hand into his hair and whimpered with need. Jack grunted, his hand now on the small of my back, pulling me close to him.

"Wait," I said, breaking the kiss. "We can't do this, Jack."

He chuckled, and lifted me onto the counter, setting me down next to my ice cream. "Of course we can. In fact, we just did, and to be honest with you, I'd really like to do that again. To be very honest with you, I want to do a whole lot more."

"*That* can't happen Jack. We work together and there are a lot of people that are counting on me...counting on *us*. So, like I said, *we can't do this.*"

"*Or*," he said grinning devilishly, "we *can* do this and not tell anyone," before once again kissing me deeply. I was lost. I'd never felt anything like when he kissed me. My mind raced as I forced myself away from him once again.

"I'm serious. I'm not into casual hookups Jack."

"Hold on, I never said anything about casual. I don't

screw around. I'm a one-woman man."

"Well, what exactly are you looking for here? A girl-friend? A fuck buddy?"

"Look, Hadley, you've been a problem since the day I met you."

"Excuse me," I said, pushing away from him. *"I'm a problem?"*

"Yes, actually, you are," he said. "I can't focus when you're around and quite frankly you're causing my work to suffer. I've wracked my brain, and I can only think of one way to solve this dilemma."

"And what is that exactly?" I challenged.

"We need to fuck."

* * *

Hadley

"What?"

"You heard me, and what's more, you agree," Jack said as he closed the distance between us.

"I do not, and you're not listening to me. *This*," I waved my hand between the two of us, "isn't going to happen."

"Not tonight, I agree." I started to speak again, but he cut me off. "But I'd like you to start thinking about when." He kissed me again and I once again felt my resolve soften. I'd always been able to resist the unwanted advances of men, but this was not unwanted and he knew it.

I stroked his bearded cheek. Damn, he was gorgeous. "I don't know, Jack," I whispered.

He kissed me again. "You are so beautiful."

"Okay, Prince Charming, let's take it down a notch, huh?"

"Prince Charming?"

"How many women does that work on?" I challenged.

Jack chuckled. "You think I'm handing you a line?"

"Big time," I said.

"No lines, baby."

"That sounds like another line," she said.

He sighed, running his hands up my thighs. I swallowed, willing myself not to react. If he kept this up, I'd rip my panties off for him and let him fuck me on Rex and Roxie's kitchen island.

"I really need you to stop doing that," I rasped.

"How come?"

I squeezed my eyes shut and whispered, "Because I like it."

"Look at me." I met his eyes and he smiled. "Let's have a little fun. You know neither of us is going to be able to think straight until we do."

Before I could protest further, I felt the words fall out of my mouth.

"Okay, but this has to happen before the tour starts. Once we hit the road, we hit the brakes on whatever this is."

"If that's what you want."

"And not here, Jack. I'm not defiling Rex and Roxie's hospitality by having sex with you in their home."

"Is the guest house included in that?"

I bit my lip. "Yes."

"Okay, you on the pill?"

I nodded.

"I'm gonna get tested and you can figure out a place while we're waiting on those results."

"Okay."

"Gonna kiss you now, Hadley."

"Okay," I whispered, and leaned to meet his mouth. Good lord, the man could kiss.

"I'm gonna head back before I can't."

"Probably a good idea," I agreed.

He kissed me one more time and I took my now melting ice cream with me back to my room. The rest of the night was spent wishing I had some kind of battery operated orgasm inducer, but I finally fell into a fitful sleep, dreaming of the man who I was sure would ruin me.

Jack

THOUGHT KISSING her might make me able to let her go. It didn't. It just made me want her more. I walked back to the guest house with all things Hadley on my mind. She obviously wasn't going to make things easy for me.

The next morning, I made my way to the main house for a cup of coffee. My coffee maker was fully operational, but Roxie had a way with roasted beans that was truly unrivalled. More importantly, I was hoping to see Hadley before I headed to the studio. Coffee had become my drug of choice once I got sober, but I was currently jonesing for a fix of Hadley. As hoped, Roxie was in the kitchen doing her magic and Rex was sitting at the island with his iPad. Unfortunately, Miss Simon was nowhere to be seen.

"Good morning." Roxie grinned. How someone could be so happy this early in the day was beyond me. "Coffee?" she asked.

"Am I that predictable?" I mused.

"The last thing anyone would ever call you is predictable, Jackie boy," Rex said without raising his eyes from his laptop.

"What are you looking at?" I asked.

"An email from Lucy. The last few tour dates have finally been locked down and she's updated the website. We are on the verge of hitting the road, my friend, and the rock world is all abuzz."

"I still can't believe so many people care about this reunion...especially since you've been out there playing these songs for years."

"You still don't get it, do you?"

"What?"

"It's not just the songs that connect with people. It's the players as well. People have been dying for you and Robbie to play these songs again. They want to see and hear the guys that wrote and recorded them. The fans missed you. We all did."

Rex was right, I didn't get it. I never thought of myself as anything special. I'm a drummer because I wanted to play drums, it's just that simple. The fact that I happened to find success was almost irrelevant to me. It's not that I don't fully appreciate the love and support of our fans; it just simply never put fuel in my tank. I loved to play and create music with people I cared about.

"I guess I never assumed anyone would listen, and I still find it very humbling that they did. I forget sometimes how big this band was."

"You mean how big we *are*. I think you should prepare yourself for what's coming Jack. Pacific is fully behind promoting the EP and the tour and almost every venue is sold out." Rex raised an eyebrow and Roxie took a long, slow sip from her mug, a sly smile on her lips. "I think I'm going to need another very strong cup to go please."

* * *

Hadley

I heard voices downstairs and just couldn't bring myself to walk down there. I was sure they'd know about the kiss and I wasn't ready for that yet. I stared at myself in the mirror and let out a quiet squeak of frustration. This was my third outfit...a pair of leggings with a long sweater and knee-high boots.

It wasn't quite what I wanted. I wanted sexy. But I wanted sexy that didn't look like I was *going* for sexy...hence my dilemma. I was one of those unfortunate souls who couldn't flirt. And, although I fully understood that flirting could be done several ways, I couldn't even wink. I just managed to look like I was trying to get sunscreen out of my eyes whenever I tried. This had given me such a complex; I just couldn't bring myself to go further on the flirting front.

I pulled off my sweater and went back into the closet. In the end, I chose a pleated skirt that ended just above my knees and looked just as cute with my boots. I grabbed my favorite off-the-shoulder sweater that I already knew Jack liked, and then brushed out my hair.

I was a little behind, but I waited until all was quiet before heading downstairs. I walked into the kitchen to grab a cup of coffee and nearly jumped out of my skin when Roxie said, "Hey, Hadley."

I didn't see her sitting at the table by the window.

"Morning."

She nodded toward the coffee pot. "Just made a fresh batch."

I let out a sigh of relief. "Thank you."

"How'd you sleep?"

"Really well," I lied as I prepared my coffee with my back to her. I could feel the heat in my cheeks as I thought about my X-rated dreams. "That bed is amazing."

"I'm glad," she said.

After taking a few deep breaths, I faced her and smiled. "What are you up to today?"

"I have to shop," she complained. "I hate shopping."

"Then why do you do it?"

"Because I love my man." She rolled her eyes. "I'm the only one he trusts when it comes to stocking him up for the road."

"Oh, I absolutely get that," I said. "Every single member of Roses wants something different, so I try to accommodate as much as possible, but sometimes they just have to suffer a little and go without."

Roxie giggled. "Rex doesn't 'go without.'"

I glanced around the room. "No, I don't suppose he does."

"You meeting Lucy today?"

"Yes." I glanced at my watch. "Sully's actually supposed—"

"Miss Simon," Sully said from the doorway of the kitchen.

I gasped nearly spilling my coffee and Roxie grinned. "Yeah, he's stealth like that."

"I'm ready," I said, rinsing my coffee cup out and putting it in the dishwasher.

"Mr. Haddon said you'll need transportation later," Sully said to Roxie.

"Yes. Maybe in an hour?"

"That'll be fine. I'll be here."

"Perfect," she said. "I'll see you later, Hadley."

"Sounds good." I grabbed my bag and followed Sully out to the car.

* * *

Jack

Rex and I arrived at the studio a little past 10:00am. The first part of our musical life together had been almost completely nocturnal, so it was still a bit strange for me to play music with Rex and Robbie during daylight hours. Like most rock bands, we'd always rehearsed, traveled, played, partied and did whatever else at night. The day time was for sleeping or radio interviews, and we didn't do radio interviews. In fact, after we started dealing with stalkers and paparazzi, we tried our best to stay away from the media as much as possible.

I scanned the parking lot for Hadley's car, but to no avail.

"Damn it," I muttered under my breath.

"What?" Rex asked

"Oh, nothing, I just realized I forgot my watch on my night stand." I hated lying to Rex, but if there was any way I was going to be with Hadley, I knew I had to keep this under very tight wraps.

As we walked into the studio, I fell back so I could slide the watch I'd just lied about off my wrist and shove it into my jeans pocket.

Most of the day was spent tightening up the set list for the tour. We'd released seven albums, so there was much material to comb through. At this point, we'd probably played through two thirds of our catalogue over the past few weeks, and were getting close to having a final song order down. The reality that I was about to be thrust back into my former life was starting to set in. It was now merely days until the madness would truly begin and I wasn't sure I was ready. My mind was swimming, and I could barely concentrate.

Where the hell is Hadley?

"Earth to Jack," Robbie's voice snapped me back to attention.

"Sorry, what?" I asked.

"What do you think of closing with Song for Steven?"

"Oh, um sure, whatever you guys think."

"Rex likes the idea, but I think it's too slow, so we need you to weigh in here. You okay?"

"Yeah, sorry, I was just someplace else for a minute. I think I agree with you, it's a little slow."

"Okay then, let's move Song for Steven to the middle of the set and close with Pages. We can leave the encores as wild cards and pick 'em each night like we used to."

"Sounds great—"

My words stopped then and there as I saw Hadley enter the control room. I immediately rose from my drum throne and made my way for the door. Rex and Robbie had their backs to the glass, so they didn't see her enter.

"Sorry guys, I need to take a quick break and get some fresh air." I rushed out of the space before my band could even respond. I entered the control room and nearly passed out. Hadley was wearing the sweater that made me want to fuck her…and a skirt that made me want to fuck her, and goddammit, she wore knee-high boots that made me want to fuck her. I'd never seen her curves so perfectly on display and it drove me crazy. Vic was sitting at the console, his back to us with headphones on. I assumed he was listening to the rough mixes of the new songs we'd been recording.

"Hey there. I missed you at the house this morning," I said.

"You were looking for me?" she asked with a shy smile.

"Well, I happened to be in the house, grabbing some

coffee..."

"Your coffee maker on the fritz?"

"No, I was just..."

"Looking for me," she said, in a soft low rasp.

"Yes."

"And now that you've found me, do you like what you see?"

My already hardening cock stiffened to the point of pain. At that very moment, I wasn't sure if I had ever been more physically attracted to someone. I wasn't just turned on. Fucking Hadley was no longer a desire, it was a need. I motioned to Vic and then to the door, and we exited out into the lobby where we were alone.

"Yes, I very much like what I see and I think you know that," I said, still careful to keep my voice down. "Does this mean, you've thought of a time and place for us?"

"Working on that." Her gorgeous smile lit up her face. Her breasts were heaving underneath the tight fabric. I wanted them in my hands. I wanted them in my mouth. I wanted to feel my hard cock between them.

"Work faster. I can't last much longer and now you're just teasing me."

"Speaking of working, isn't there someplace you should be right now?"

"Besides between your thighs?" I leaned in for a quick kiss.

"Ohmigod, stop it." She stepped out of reach. "Someone'll see us! Besides, I have to get going. I only stopped by to drop off some documents for Rex to sign and then I have other work to tend to all day."

"Are you sure that's the only reason you stopped by?" I challenged.

"Okay, maybe not the only reason, but I really do have to get these to Rex, and get going."

"Will you meet me back here later tonight? Everyone

will still be around, but we could have a coffee together or something."

"I'll see what I can do. I'll text you later and let you know how my schedule looks."

"Just have your people contact my people."

She smiled. "I'm not sure how that'll work since Lucy is your 'people' and I'm Roses for Anna's 'people,'"

"That does pose a dilemma. Alright then, text me and I hope to see you later."

I guided her gently to the back wall and kissed her...taking my time. She smelled amazing, and I felt her heart racing as I held her to my chest.

She pushed me away and took a wobbly footed step around me. "You *have* to stop doing that!"

"I'll stop doing it when you stop getting all hot and bothered by it."

She licked her lips and handed me a manila envelope. "Give this to Rex, please."

"When do you need it back?"

"Tonight would be good."

I grinned, nodding slowly. "An excuse to come back."

"Jack," she admonished.

"Yeah, baby?"

She jabbed a finger toward me and shook her head. "Stop it."

I chuckled and she gave me a lingering look before walking out the door. I turned around and headed back into the control room. Vic looked like he hadn't moved an inch from his spot and Robbie and Rex were still in the tracking room pouring over the show details. Even though we were keeping our staging, lights and video production relatively simple, there were still many last-minute items to iron out. I knew the last thing my band needed was for their drummer to be distracted by a woman, but it was all I could do to keep my thoughts from her.

"Hadley dropped this by," I said as I walked back into the room.

Rex took the envelope and ripped it open. "Cool. When does she need 'em back?"

"Tonight."

"I'll look at them when we break for dinner. You ready to get back at it?"

"Sure thing. Let's run through the first three songs and get all the transitions as tight as possible," I said. I grabbed my sticks and sat down behind my kit, staring blankly into space.

"There he goes again." Robbie said.

"You okay, Jackie? You seem a little distracted again today. Everything alright?" Rex asked.

"Sorry. I haven't been getting much sleep. Guess it's nerves or something."

"Roxie and I thought we heard you down in the kitchen last night."

"Yeah, I was. I...uh...was grabbing some of that tea she buys for me."

Rex studied me for a moment. This was not good. Rex Haddon had the best bullshit meter of anyone I'd ever known. If I wasn't very careful I was going to blow this thing (whatever it was) with Hadley.

Rex nodded. "Good, I'm glad it worked. God knows you're going to need some rest before we hit the road."

Rest was the farthest thing from my mind right now. I didn't know what the fuck was wrong with me. I was about to embark on the first tour in what felt like forever, and I was secretly running around chasing tail. The only thoughts scarier than the ones about the tour ahead of me, were the ones I had about Hadley. Pam was the last, and only, woman that had ever made me feel like this and she was the love of my life. There was no way in hell I could or would ever entertain thoughts of love, but I knew I wanted her more than anyone since Pam, and that thought alone was driving me insane.

"If you ladies are done with your little cozy time tea chat, can we please get back to playing some fucking music?"

The boys chuckled and we got back to it.

CHAPTER
EIGHT

Jack

AFTER THE DAY'S rehearsals were done, we broke for dinner and ironed out more of the final tour details. We'd be hitting the road in a little under a week and musically and personally we were firing on all cylinders. After dinner, we said our goodbyes and headed for home, but I had other plans.

"I left my headphones back at the studios, so I'm gonna run and grab those real quick. I'll see you back at the house," I said to Rex. Hadley and I had traded texts throughout the day and we had decided to meet up at ten o'clock.

"See you back at the homestead then." Rex smiled and waved as he drove away.

After stopping at the store for protection, I got to the studio just after ten but Hadley was nowhere to be found. The parking lot was empty and all the lights were out.

Shit, she's chickened out and she's not coming.

Moments later, I saw headlights coming toward the parking lot and my heart began to race. Hadley climbed out of the cab and the air left my lungs. She was stunning.

"Sorry I'm late. I wasn't sure what you'd be in the mood for, so I brought a few options," she said smiling and holding up a cardboard drink holder, loaded with assorted coffee and tea.

"Thanks, but I'm not really in the mood for anything on that tray. I'm only interested in the one who's carrying it."

I walked over to her, set the tray on the hood of my truck and kissed her slowly and deeply. Her hands went to my cheeks and I pulled her closer, deepening my kisses. My tongue was eager to explore her entire body.

"Let's go inside," I said, guiding her to the front door.

We entered the lobby and I keyed in the security code, then turned on a single lamp near the reception area. I made sure the doors were locked again and the building was empty before sitting on the sofa and pulling her onto my lap.

"I thought we were just meeting for coffee. Did you lure me here under false pretenses?" she teased.

"I couldn't wait any longer."

She straddled me and smiled as she leaned down to kiss me. "And I don't want you to wait any longer."

She tasted like caramel and mint and it drove me mad.

Sliding my hands under her sweater, I cupped her lace-covered breasts, then tugged the material down and rolled her nipples into tight buds.

She whimpered, dropping her head back and pressing

further into my hands. Her quiet mews encouraged me to go further and I slid her sweater over her head, dropping it to the floor before unhooking her bra.

Fuck, once her tits were free, I nearly came. "Gorgeous, baby."

She focused on me with hooded eyes and licked her lips. "Please talk less."

I chuckled, sliding my hands up her thighs and ripping the thin strip of lace keeping me from her pussy.

She gasped. "I liked those panties."

"I'll buy you more," I promised, and cupped her mound, sliding my fingers into her.

She rocked against my palm and dropped her head back again, which gave me access to her neck and I took full advantage.

Kissing my way down her chest, I sucked a nipple into my mouth, then another, biting gently as I felt her soak my hand.

"I can't wait, Jack," she rasped, so I shifted so I could get a condom on, then guided her onto my cock.

I nearly lost my load and had to take a few breaths. I felt like a fuckin' teenager. "Fuck," I breathed out.

"So good," she whispered, anchoring her hands on my shoulders and lifting herself slightly before sliding back down.

I cupped her breasts and rolled her nipples again while she continued to impale herself. Her tight, wet pussy encased my dick and it felt better than anything I'd ever experienced before.

When I knew I couldn't wait, I guided her off my lap, pressing her back to the sofa, while keeping us connected, then slammed into her.

"Oh, God, yes, Jack!" she panted.

I couldn't wait. She just felt so fucking good, so I came, but worked her clit until I felt her walls contract around me.

I kissed her again, gently pulling out of her before wrapping the condom in a tissue and throwing it in the plastic bag from the store. I stretched out beside Hadley again and pulled her close. "I liked that," I said, and kissed her forehead.

She smiled. "Me too."

I slid my hand to her ass and cupped her. "I like this most of all."

She slid a leg over my thigh, pressing her pussy to my dick. "Yeah?"

"Yeah," I confirmed, kissing her again. "Fuckin' sexy as hell."

"I like that you think I'm sexy."

"Well, that's a fact, baby, rather than opinion."

She smiled, stroking my beard. "You're really charming when you want to be, huh?"

"Just bein' honest."

She kissed me gently. "We should get back."

"In a minute."

She rolled her eyes. "What did you tell Rex you were doing?"

"Grabbing my headphones," I said. "What was your excuse?"

"I was at Lucy's so I just told her I was heading home. I had more of a problem losing Sully. But I grabbed the taxi before he could catch me."

I chuckled. "I'll drop you back, then."

"Um, no you won't," she countered. "I'll grab a cab or an über or something."

"Hadley."

"Jack," she mimicked. "Look, if this is going to work, we have to be careful."

I sighed. She was right. I didn't like it, but I had to agree that she had a point. I sat up and pulled my clothes back on. "I'll wait while we call you a car, then I'm following you back."

"Fine." She rolled her eyes. "Are you always like this?"

"Like what?"

"Bossy."

I smiled helping her off the sofa. "I protect what's mine, Hadley."

She shook her head. "Okay, handsome, let's take it down a notch, huh? This"—she waved a hand between us—"is a fling. Before the tour officially starts, this will be officially over. I don't belong to you."

I forced down panic while she dressed. Again, she was right. It's what we'd agreed to, but now that I'd fucked her, I didn't think I'd ever let her go. For the moment, though, I'd keep that to myself.

"Call your car," I grumbled and stepped into the tracking room to grab my headphones.

* * *

Hadley

I'd excused myself to head to bed just before ten. Jack had followed me (and the confused looking über driver) home, but hadn't come into the house, and I kind of missed him. Silly, considering I'd seen him just a few hours earlier, but I liked him. Liked his energy, so the fact I wouldn't see him again until the morning kind of bummed me out.

I'd been between tossing and turning for about twenty minutes when I felt the bed dip and sat up with a frightened gasp.

"It's me baby," Jack whispered wrapping an arm around my waist.

I flicked on the lamp next to the bed and faced him with frown. "*What* are you doing in here?"

He tugged me onto his chest, kissing me deeply. "Missed you."

"You scared me half to death."

"Sorry baby, let me make it up to you."

"That's another thing. You can't call me ba—"

Before I could object further, he tugged my T-shirt off and drew a nipple into his mouth, biting down gently. I arched into his touch as he continued to shower attention on my breasts while sliding a hand under the waistband of my panties and between my legs. His finger slid through the wetness and then slipped inside of me. I groaned and pushed against him as he slid another inside. His thumb found my clit and I moaned. I could feel my orgasm building, but before it washed over me, he removed his hand.

"Jack," I whispered as he stood. "Where are you going?"

He pushed his pjs from his hips and removed his shirt. God, he was magnificent. After he slid my panties from my hips, he rolled on a condom and rose up above me, settling his hips between mine and guiding himself inside of me. I wrapped my legs around him and arched up.

"Fuck, baby." He slid out of me and then back in slowly. "God, you feel so good."

"More, Jack."

He covered my mouth with his and thrust deep inside of me.

"Yes," I whispered against his lips.

His tongue slid into my mouth as his cock surged deeper and deeper, faster and faster. I broke the kiss and moaned. "Yes!" I called out.

"Shhh," he warned, in a whisper.

"We really shouldn't be doing this here, Jack."

"You want me to stop?"

I shook my head. "Hell, no."

"Then you need to be quiet."

He thrust back into me and I felt my orgasm build and relished the feeling, but when his hand slid between us and his finger found my clit, it was over and I exploded around him. I forced myself not to scream.

Within seconds, I felt Jack's cock pulsate inside of me and he kissed my neck as he rolled us onto our sides. "I'll make that last a little longer next time."

I broke our connection, then rolled to face him. "We can't do this here."

He grinned. "We just did."

I squeezed my eyes shut and shook my head.

"Eyes, Had."

I focused on him again and sighed. "You're a really bad influence."

He kissed me and I found myself sliding my hands into his hair. It took several minutes to come to my senses and break the kiss and whisper, "Jack."

"I can't *not* see you, Hadley."

I ran my thumb over his bottom lip and he bit it gently. I felt it all the way to my clit. "I like that, Jack, but we leave tomorrow..."

"Come to my hotel room tomorrow night."

"But we were supposed to get this out of our systems and end things before the tour started. That was the deal Jack."

"I'm renegotiating our deal," he said.

"Maybe I'll come by."

"I'll rephrase," he said, sliding his hand between my legs again. "I want you in my room no later than midnight."

I licked my lips and rocked against his palm. "I—"

"Midnight, Hadley. Say it."

"Midnight," I said. "I'll be there."

He climbed off the bed and pulled my body to the edge, sliding my legs over his shoulders. I shifted as his mouth kissed his way down the inside of my left thigh. He gripped both of mine and found my eyes. "Don't move. Got me?"

I nodded as I took a deep breath and bit my lip, dropping my head back to the mattress. He lowered his mouth to my clit and sucked until I couldn't help myself from bucking my hips. He gripped my thighs tighter and lowered my bottom to the bed, spreading my knees. I whimpered as he sucked harder, slipping a finger inside of me. I slid my hand into his hair and arched against his mouth.

Without warning, he tugged me further down the bed, and slammed into me. I forced myself not to cry out and arched again.

"Too much, baby?" he asked.

"God, no. Harder."

He grasped my thighs again, holding them against his hips and lifting me slightly as he surged into me. I fisted my hands in the comforter, unable to do much else because he had me anchored to his body. He thrust into me again and again, his body locked as he held me to him. I came around him, but didn't have time to enjoy it as I was flipped onto my stomach and taken from behind.

I steadied myself on all fours and Jack reached around me to cup my breasts. His movements were slower now, which only managed to drive me crazy. "You okay?"

I pressed back into him. "Yes."

He squeezed my leg gently. "Spread, Hadley."

I spread and his hand left my breast and found my clit. I groaned, grinding against him. He slid in slowly again and I sighed. "Yes."

Jack slammed into me again and I shoved my face in the pillow and screamed. His thrusts came harder until I exploded around him, then he surged in two more times and I felt his cock pulse as he came inside of me. He kissed my lower back and then my bottom, before sliding out of me and heading to the bathroom to get rid of the condom.

I let my body fall to the mattress, my legs nothing but jelly, and smiled as he returned to the bed. "Amazing," I whispered.

He leaned over me and smiled. "I better get back."

"Okay."

He kissed me gently, then grabbed his discarded clothing off the floor. "I got tested yesterday," he said as he pulled on his pants.

I leaned up on my forearms. "For?"

"For everything. I should get the results before we leave. You *are* on the pill, right?"

"Yes. I told you that already." I sat up. "Do you want *me* to get tested?"

"When's the last time you were with someone?"

"Over a year."

"Were you clean then?"

"Gross." I wrinkled my nose. "Yes, I was clean."

He grinned, tugging on his shirt. "Then I think we're good."

"So romantic," I deadpanned, flopping back onto the pillows.

Jack chuckled, sitting on the edge of the bed and kissing me gently. "I don't want anything between us. You're too beautiful not to feel all of you."

I swallowed. Well, that was seriously sweet. "That sounds good, actually."

He stroked my cheek. "Yeah?"

I nodded.

"Good. I'll see you tomorrow."

I nodded again, then he kissed me and sneaked out of my room and I was left sated, but wanting more...a lot more.

CHAPTER
NINE

Jack

THE MOMENT I'M officially 'on the road' is one
of my favorite feelings in the world. I love being in
the studio, rehearsing and writing, but it's all for
nothing if we don't get out and play for the people.
Being in motion soothes my soul. Once the band was over,
I'd lost myself in travel. I suppose a part of me doesn't
know how to stay in one place for too long.

"You ready, Jackie boy?" Rex asked as we began rolling.

Rex had tricked out our old tour bus years ago, and even
though it had a couple of bunk beds and a private bedroom

and bathroom, we needed more creature comforts now that we were older and sober, so we'd negotiated (well, Lucy had) for the label to pay for hotel rooms for the bands and their families. Touring these days was a much smaller affair with much smaller budgets. RatHound was footin' the bill for the crew and roadies for both bands (that part Hadley had negotiated so Roses for Anna didn't have to pay). In the end, it worked out better for us financially and it meant I could have Hadley to myself.

"Ready as I'll ever be." I smiled. "Thanks for this, Rex."

"Thank me? You're the one who made this tour possible, by saying yes. There was no way we were going to go out without you."

"Fuckin' A," Robbie added.

"To the band," I said raising my plastic water bottle for a toast.

I was joined by the others with an unsatisfying dull clacking of plastic, a reminder that the days of champagne and blow were long gone.

Our first show was tomorrow night in Portland and I couldn't wait to hit the stage. My passion for music had been reignited by the faith of my best friend and my passion for just about everything else was off the charts thanks to Hadley, who was currently behind us in the Roses for Anna bus.

I shot her a text. *Wish you were here.*

See you at the first pit stop ;)

The mood on the bus was electric. Spirits had never been higher in the RatHound camp and it was great to be back on the road with so many familiar faces. Lucy was doing an amazing job as the band's new manager and she was able to hire several key members from our original tech crew including Teddy and Spike, who we'd dubbed "The Road Hounds" back in the day. They were amazing roadies and certifiably insane.

Teddy, who had now been promoted to stage manager, was a very large man, and not to be trifled with. Spike was a skinny, pale little runt—they were a sort of Laurel and Hardy of their trade. Teddy was now missing his left pinky and eye due to a pyrotechnic malfunction while touring with the Clergy, a band we knew well from back in the day. We joked and told him even though he'd been promoted, we'd have to pay him less now since there was, well, less of *him* these days.

Spike was serving as our bus driver, and as was tradition, driving the first hundred miles naked as a jaybird. This may have been our fist sober tour, but I had a feeling it was going to be far from boring.

"Come on Spike, you pasty sonofabitch, get this bus moving!" Robbie yelled as the bus engine roared. Music, laughter and plenty of stories from our past filled the bus as we drove through the night.

* * *

Hadley

"Boyfriend?" Ray asked, sitting next to me at the little banquette in the bus.

"Hmm?"

He nodded toward my phone gripped in my hands.

"Oh." I felt heat in my cheeks. "No. Just working on some last-minute details."

Ray Samuels was Bam's drum tech. He had been a roadie for the band for over five years, and was a trusted member of their camp. He was nice, but a little too much in my space at times. He'd always had boundary issues when it came to me and I was fixin' to either say something to him…or make Bam do it. However, for the moment, I was stuck with him hovering because I wasn't interested in making things tense on the first day of the tour.

"You excited?"

I nodded. "I am. How about you?"

"Shit, yeah. Total access to RatHound? Never thought that would ever happen."

"I know." I smiled. "It's kind of a mind-bend."

"Totally. It's gonna be a great tour, I'm stoked."

I smiled and nodded, and saw him slide, ever so closer, to me.

"Yeah, so I guess we'll be...uh, seeing each other around," I said.

Real smooth.

He continued. "So, if there's anything you need, you just let me know. Anything at all."

He shot me what I assumed was supposed to be a sexy 'come hither' look, and it took every ounce of my strength to contain my laughter.

"Okay, thanks," was all I could squeak out.

"Had, can I talk to you a minute?" Bam asked, and I excused myself from the table and walked to the back of the bus to sit next to him.

"What's up?" I asked.

"You just looked like you needed saving."

I giggled. "This is why you're my favorite."

"Do I need to have a conversation?"

"Not yet," I said. "He hasn't done anything that would warrant it."

"You let me know."

"I will, buddy." I smiled and leaned back against the seat.

What I really wanted to do, was tell Jack. It was as if I had some sort of teenage urge to "go tell my boyfriend" that some little creep was hitting on me, but Jack wasn't my boyfriend, and I certainly shouldn't be thinking of him like that. I simply couldn't turn my thoughts away from him, or help the way I was feeling.

I changed the subject. "You missing Lucy?"

Lucy was traveling with RatHound, but I didn't know how long that would last because they were both ridiculously attached to one another.

"Yeah," he admitted, and waved his cell phone. "Thank God for texting."

I giggled. "Well, she and I could always swap. We're going to be together for six weeks, and we're essentially doing everything together, so why doesn't she travel with you and I'll travel with them?"

I wasn't about to admit the real reason for my suggestion.

"That's not a bad idea. I'll talk to her," Bam said.

"Sounds good, just let me know."

We drove in relative silence for the next hour, arriving at the amphitheater just before one. Being a little claustrophobic, I was ready to get off the bus, so I rose to my feet as soon as the brake was set.

"I'm going to meet Lucy," I said to no one in particular, and rushed off the bus.

Walking into the hot Ridgefield sun, I took a deep breath. I loved the Pacific Northwest. Not as much as home, but definitely a close second.

Lucy walked toward me with a huge grin on her face. "You ready?"

I looked around, hoping to spot Jack, but to no avail. I hoped he was as excited as I was about opening night, but not as nervous as I was.

"So ready," I lied, and we made our way to meet with the venue manager and Jimbo Reno, the concert promoter that was backing most of the tour. My feet froze after five confident strides. "Lucy, what if I'm not actually ready? What if I'm terrified?"

"Terrified of what?"

"Of everyone knowing how new I am as a manager?" I

whispered. "What if I make a fool of myself in front of this guy?"

"Jimbo?" Lucy chuckled. "You're afraid of embarrassing yourself in front of Jimbo Reno? When you meet him, you're going to see how funny that is."

"No, not just Jimbo...*all* the Jimbos. I feel like any minute Bam and the band are going to tap me on the shoulder and tell me they've made a horrible mistake in choosing me as their manager, and that I'm being replaced."

"Sweetie, you're spiraling." Lucy put a hand on each of my shoulders and looked at me in a way that reminded me of her father, a man that could truly charm anyone into a relaxed and pliable state.

"Don't you 'Rex' me, Lucy Nelson. I'm serious."

"I am too. What you're feeling is totally normal. This is your first tour as the band's manager, but this is *not* your first tour. You know these people and you know this world. Nothing has changed, except that you don't have to go through Chas to get your job done. This is your show now, and it's show time." She made 'jazz hands' and I couldn't help but laugh.

"That's better. C'mon, let's go show these stinky boys who's in charge," Lucy said, hooking her arm into mine, leading us toward our destination.

Even though Lucy was younger and technically less experienced than me, she had a deep knowledge of the business and people that I admired. I trusted her judgment and valued her opinion. I'd spent most of my life around boys and it was nice to be forming such a close bond with a woman I admired.

After a few twists and turns we found the office of Kurt Varney, manager of the Sofa King Amphitheater, and entered to find him sharing a drink with the aforementioned Jimbo Reno. Jimbo was undoubtedly the biggest concert promoter on the west coast, and he had a well-earned reputation as a being a very tough guy.

"Lucy, my dear! Come here and give your Uncle Jimbo a hug and a kiss!" The hulking man, rose to his feet and embraced Lucy before she could even extend her arms, causing her to momentarily temporarily disappear from sight altogether.

"Jimbo, I can't breathe," Lucy wheezed.

He released her and stood back a pace. "My god, look how you've grown. I still remember when you were a little girl and your dad almost missed your birthday. He was on tour at the time and had to borrow my plane to make it home on time," he said, puffing up his massive chest proudly.

"And this beautiful young lady must be—" Kurt asked.

"Hadley Simon, with Roses for Anna," I said, thrusting my hand out in the most business-like way I could. I shook Kurt's hand, then Jimbo's. Jimbo's giant mitt covered mine entirely, and I was instantly pulled in for the same bear hug style assault.

"Of course you are!" Jimbo bellowed. "You ladies are just in time to join me and Kurt here for a drink. We're toasting to open night. I know your daddy gave up the sauce, so I figured I'd knock one back for him."

As his adopted surname suggested, Jim Reno "made his bones" in Nevada and most certainly bankrolled his early endeavors with mob money. He was a legitimate entertainment tycoon now, but I was all too familiar with his type. Jimbo and RatHound had major history and they trusted him, but after what I had just gone through with the band's previous manager, I wasn't about to drop my guard, no matter how charming he was. Kurt Varney lacked any and all the warmth that Jimbo had. "Please ladies, do join us," he said, in a tone that made my flesh crawl.

"Thank you, gentlemen, but we need to get back to our bands. We just wanted to stop by and make sure you didn't have any questions about our riders and collect our passes," Lucy said.

Every venue on a tour is supplied with a rider from each band, which is simply a list of needs. The band's rider contains everything from technical requirements for their staging and lighting, to what kind of salad dressing they want at dinner. Reviewing the rider was a way of making sure the band's needs are truly being met. In the eighties, Van Halen famously asked for a bowl of M&M's backstage, with all the brown candies removed. This seemed like the ultimate in rock star spoiled excess, but it was actually a shrewd business move that ensured the promoters had actually read the band's entire contract carefully.

"C'mon, surely you can have one little drink with us," Kurt continued. He was clearly many drinks into the bottle, probably in a feeble attempt to keep up with Jimbo. He was a pasty, thin, balding man with undoubtedly the worst comb-over I'd ever seen. In fact, I couldn't tell exactly where his hair was being combed over from.

"Uh, no, that's okay," I said.

"It's opening night," Kurt countered, his hot, boozy breath hanging in the air, making me feel sick. "One little drink."

Lucy smiled. "Like Uncle Jimbo said, we're a dry camp these days, so we'll have to take a rain check."

Jimbo changed the subject. "I heard you got married."

"Sure did," Lucy said smiling. She quickly held up her left hand to reveal her wedding ring.

"To *your* drummer, isn't that right?" He turned to me.

"Also correct," I said.

"I don't see on ring on *your* pretty finger," Kurt said. It was all I could do to keep from throwing up. I was willing to cut this bozo a little slack, given his current state of intoxication, and certainly didn't want to make waves on the first night out.

"Nope, just married to my work," I smiled. "And my massive gun collection."

Kurt's smile dropped, and after a few moments of dead silence, Jimbo erupted into laughter.

"Oh, I like her. I like her a lot, Lucy. Come on, ladies, let's get you those passes and make sure you guys have got everything you need."

Once all our administrative ducks had been lined up and accounted for, we headed back to the busses. I was surprised to see Jack walking toward us.

"Everything okay?" I asked as he approached us.

"Yeah, I was just checking to see if you two needed any help. You were gone for a while."

"Were you worried about us, Uncle Jack? You're so sweet," Lucy said.

Sweet indeed. As a matter of fact, I wanted to lick every inch of the man's body then and there.

"We were just getting the passes and press packets from 'drunk and drunker' in there." I said, before realizing I'd just tattled on the promoters.

"Did they give you any trouble?" Jack asked, the tone of his voice low and lethal.

"No, no. Nothing like that, they were just funny. Nothing to worry about, really."

"We can handle ourselves just fine, Uncle Jack," Lucy added.

"Of that, I have no doubt at all." He smiled, but the mirth didn't reach his eyes. "I just wanted to make sure you're okay."

In that moment, I decided not to say anything to Jack about Ray hitting on me, or Kurt's proposed soiree. Jack was clearly the protective type, and the last thing we needed was him blowing our cover by losing his cool.

"We're great. Besides, it's my job to make sure you have everything you need, not the other way around," Lucy said smiling. "You're going to have to get used to me taking care of things for you for a change."

"Fair enough," Jack smiled.

I smiled to myself. It was Lucy's job to take care of him now, but I planned on taking care of him later.

Jack

SITTING BACKSTAGE, WARMING up on my practice pad, I was struck with how comfortable I felt. All my initial fears and anxiety about the tour were completely gone and I was actually looking forward to playing. It was opening night and less than two hours until show time.

Because Lucy knew us so well, and because she was a genius, she knew we needed to ease back into the insanity that goes along with a tour, so she'd been very careful to limit press interviews and fan meet and greets before the shows. This gave us a little more time to relax and focus before hitting the stage—not that I was doing either.

Hadley was currently in our dressing room speaking with Lucy about the concessions' contract with the venue, but I couldn't focus on her words—only her mouth. I wanted that mouth on mine; I wanted it to kiss my body, to take the fullness of my cock into it. I shifted in my seat, and continued to tap away on my practice pad as she walked toward me.

"Do you warm up every time before you...play?" she asked in a whisper as she passed by.

I winked. "I always like to warm things up when I have the time."

She walked away and I tried to put her out of my mind...if only for the moment. I had to focus if I was going to get through tonight in one piece. Rex was the nicest guy in the world, but he always ran a tight ship on stage. Rex has to pull triple duty when we play live. He's singing, playing bass, and the most consistently engaged with the audience. For him to do what he does every night he needed Robbie and me to be on the money at all times.

Rex always heard everything and had his head on a swivel. The last thing any of us wanted to see on stage was what Robbie and I called the 'death ray.' I hated letting Rex down, and if I fucked up bad enough for him to shoot me the death ray, it would mean I fucked up royally.

On our last tour, I saw the death ray every night...multiple times a show. I was a strung-out mess and could barely function, let alone play well. I felt gratitude to be sitting backstage with my band again, because I didn't think it would ever happen.

How often does someone a second chance?

As I continued to warm up my hands, my thoughts were interrupted by the sound of singing—beautiful singing, in four-part harmony, coming from the adjoining dressing room. Roses for Anna was about to go on, so I figured they must be warming up.

A hush came over our dressing room as their voices rose, and I leaned back in my chair quietly unlocking and opening the door in the shared wall. The sound that poured from their room instantly gave me chills. This was music, real music, sung by young men who believed in its power. We waited for them to finish, in complete, stunned silence, and erupted into applause when they were done. The band, who were gathered together in a tight circle, spun around in surprise.

"Awww, come on man, you guys are too much," their lead singer Zeke said, bowing to his newly found audience. "Thank you."

I locked eyes with Bam, smiled and waved him over. I saw him look over at Lucy and smile shyly before making his way into our dressing room.

"Hey Jack, how's it goin'?"

I stood up and extended my hand. "Hey man, that sounded amazing. Do you guys do that shit on stage?"

"The circle of fear?" he asked.

"The what?"

"That's what we call it. It's our pre-show ritual," he explained. "It's how we connect before we go on stage."

"Well, you should bring that on stage with you."

Bam smiled wide and thanked me. I wished him a good show and returned to my warm up. I was looking forward to seeing Roses for Anna play, but didn't say so. I knew the guy looked up to me and didn't want to rattle his brain any more than it probably was. As an opening band, you had to play in front of your idols all the time, and it can be hell.

Hadley circled back into the room one last time to make sure all of her guys were ready to go. Before she left the room, she shot me a sly grin that caused a familiar buzz and I was struck with a thought: Hadley Simon was quickly becoming my new drug of choice.

* * *

Holy shit, these guys can play! "They're pretty good," I said, leaning in close to Hadley. I could smell her, and it was driving me insane. "Pretty good?" She raised both eyebrows. "I think the word you're looking for is amazing." "Yeah, alright." I smiled, but looked away before anyone spotted us staring for too long. "I should...I..." "Get going?" Hadley teased.

I mouthed, "I'll see you later," and went off to join my bandmates, who had gathered to watch the show from the other side of the stage.

"Well, they're certainly singing for their supper, aren't they?" Rex asked.

"They're fucking great!" I agreed.

"Yup."

"We're going to have to kick some major ass going on after these guys every night," Robbie said.

Rex and I turned toward one another.

"Yup," Rex said again.

I loved outdoor summer shows. Tonight, we were playing what the music industry calls a 'shed,' which are corporate owned amphitheaters that seat around fifteen to twenty thousand people. This one was located in southern Washington, just outside of Portland, Oregon and was sold out. Roses for Anna was currently playing to a half-filled venue, but I had a feeling as word got out among our fans, that wouldn't be the case for long.

"Mr. Henry." I felt a hand tap my shoulder and turned to see a young man with a bright yellow vest and a walkie-talkie. "You have an urgent call holding for you in the business office, can you follow me sir?"

"A call? What's this about?" I asked.

"I'm not sure sir, I was just asked to come and get you."

"I'm in the middle of watching a show, man, can it wait?"

"I was told to tell you the call is from Tabitha, and that it's urgent."

"I don't know anyone named...wait, did she say Tabitha or *Tabeetha*?" I asked.

"Sorry sir, yes it was Tabeetha."

Rex and Robbie looked at me puzzled.

"Sorry guys, I've gotta take this."

"Who's Tabeetha?" Rex asked.

I began following my guide and yelled out, "She's my... aunt. She's...very sick. I'll catch up with you guys in a bit."

We made our way to the offices and I was led to a small windowless room.

"Here you are, sir, your call is waiting inside," my guide said, his young face turning beet red.

"Thanks, man," I said and palmed him a twenty.

I opened the door and Hadley was sitting on top of an old desk. Sitting next to her was a small lamp that provided the only light in the room.

I grinned. "I was told I had a call from Tabeetha."

"Oh, I'm sorry. There must have been some sort of mistake. There's no phone in here, just...me."

Hadley luring me into her little trap was too much. I should have been focusing on the show, but all I could see was Hadley. Everything else around us was in darkness, but I could see her in the light, and that was all that mattered right now. I smiled slowly. "I like you better."

She giggled, reaching for me and tugging me forward. "I just need a little somethin' to tide me over."

"You want me to fuck you in the business office?" I challenged. "Kinky."

"No! Gross. Public isn't my style, but I'd be really happy with a little necking time."

I chuckled. "Just how old *are* you?"

"Ninety-four next month. I look good, huh?"

"So good." I leaned down and kissed her gently. "You do okay on the bus?"

She nodded. "Bam was missing Lucy though."

"Yeah, she was missin' him too."

"I told him I'd be willing to switch with her...you know, take one for the team."

I stroked her neck. "Take one for the team, huh?"

She smiled and nodded. "I figured she and I are doing the same job, so we can support both bands. Is that okay?"

"It poses a little problem for me."

"Crap," she whispered, dropping her gaze to the floor. "I should have talked to you about it. I'm really sorry, Jack."

I lifted her chin and kissed her again. "Not mad about it, Hadley...just gonna make it harder for me not to drag you into the tiny bathroom and fuck you senseless."

"I didn't really think about that." She licked her lips and smiled. "Can you control yourself?"

"Considering you'll be in my hotel bed whenever possible."

"I can't be in your bed every night. Someone will see."

I kissed her again, sliding my hand under her shirt and tugging her bra down in order to roll her nipple between my fingers.

She arched into my touch. "Jack."

"Yeah, baby?" I whispered, leaning down to kiss her again.

"God, that feels so good."

I removed my hand and she whimpered.

"You gonna sleep with me every night you can?" I challenged.

She wrinkled her nose. "Maybe."

I fixed her bra and shirt and stepped back. "Yeah?"

"Come back," she said with a groan.

"You gonna sleep with me every night?" I repeated. She rolled her eyes. "Fine. Yes, evil one, I will." I grinned and closed the distance between us again. "Good answer."

She stroked my beard. "FYI, I don't really like blackmail."

I chuckled. "Noted."

"But I like what you were just doing."

"I'll make it up to you tonight and do that again." She grinned, kissing me gently. "FYI, I like that kind of apology."

"Noted." I kissed her quickly one last time. "Alright, sweet face, we really do have to go before someone notices we're *both* missing. I'm sure my band is anxiously awaiting an update on the health status of my dear aunt Tabeetha."

Hadley burst into laughter and as I held her, I couldn't remember the last time I'd been so happy and at peace.

* * *

"Fuck! Fuck! Fuck!" I couldn't remember the last time I'd been so panicked and full of fear. My ears were ringing from the near-deafening screeching that had shot through my in-ear monitors moments earlier. "What the fuck, Teddy?"

"They're trying to figure out what's going on, boss!" Teddy yelled back.

Back in the day, musicians only had giant speakers on the floor and to the sides of the stage to hear ourselves. It was a primitive solution that did damage to the hearing of many great players and singers. Over ten years ago, in-ear monitoring had become the industry standard, allowing musicians to have custom molded, super high-quality ear buds made in order to hear themselves much better, at significantly lower volume. Apparently, our monitoring system had some bugs to be worked out, and just three minutes before we were to start playing, I found myself unable to hear anything but eardrum-crushing noise.

"Tell them to figure it out fast!"

I looked over at Rex and his death ray was locked on several members of the band's sound crew, who were currently in a state of mild panic.

I heard one of them call out, "We're rebooting the monitoring desk now."

Our show opened with a three-minute video piece that served as a snap shot of the band's history. It was filled with old photos, video clips, soundbites and reminders of our past. We were about one minute from when I was to count off the first song, and the digital mixing board that controlled the band's entire monitor feed was being powered back up after a full shut down.

"This'd better fuckin' work or we're in for a long night," Robbie said.

I looked to my left and awaited the all clear sign from the monitor station. There was nothing like last minute technical chaos to get the adrenaline pumping. I needed to slow down my breathing and mentally clear myself or I'd go blazing into the first song way too fast.

I glanced to my right and saw Hadley standing with Lucy, a look of concern on her face. She must have seen me pull my in-ears out and could clearly see we were having major technical issues.

I smiled and mouthed, "I'm okay," just in time to get the thumbs up from our monitoring engineer. This was it. After years of absolute silence, RatHound was about to make a very big noise.

I heard the crescendo of the opening video's music and quickly popped my in-ears back in just before the massive curtain that had been hiding us from the audience dropped. I took a deep breath, steadied myself. Much like Dorothy, I clicked my sticks together a few times and found myself going back home.

CHAPTER
ELEVEN

Hadley

AS JACK STARTED to play, my heartbeat returned to normal. I don't fully know why I was so worried. Roses for Anna's set had gone perfectly and they'd played better than they ever had, so I shouldn't be concerned about RatHound. But the reality was, Jack had weaseled his way into my heart, and now I felt his irritation and wanted to fix whatever ailed him.

Lucy rushed up to me and stared toward her father. Rex caught her eye and smiled as he gave her a quick nod, and Lucy let out a breath of relief. "Holy crap on a stick, I thought someone was going to lose their head."

I nodded. "Yeah. I don't understand what happened between Roses set."

"I have no idea, but Teddy's gonna have to give me some answers...before they finish their last song."

"I hope this isn't an omen."

Lucy gasped. "Don't *say* that."

I grimaced. "Sorry." I glanced at Jack just as he looked at me and let me know he was okay.

God, the man was sexy. His long hair hung past his shoulders, and the mere sight of him sitting behind his drums made my body ache for him.

"I'm going to check on the guys," I said, and attempted to force myself away from Jack. "Do you need anything?"

"You're leaving now? Don't you want to see their set?" Lucy asked.

Of course I did, but I felt like all eyes were on me. I was trying to keep this thing between me and Jack a secret, but imagined cartoon hearts swirling over my head, and was pretty sure everyone could see them as well.

"I just want to make sure my guys don't need anything."

"They'll be fine. Besides, you know as well as I do, they'll be right here to watch the show any minute."

As if on cue, Bam, Zeke, Jimmy, and Edward appeared. They had changed out of their sweat soaked stage clothes and shared the same wide-eyed look as everyone else in the sold-out crowd that night—slightly stunned and ready to see their heroes take the stage.

The venue lights darkened and the now filled to capacity venue went crazy. Jack counted the band off and they went tearing into a song from their very first album.

My emotions were warring with my mind and I couldn't stop myself from glancing to my left, nervous that everyone could read my body language. I shouldn't have been concerned, the rest of the group, including Lucy (who'd seen her dad play a million times), was engrossed in the music, so I let myself feel everything Jack was emitting.

Bad idea.

I suddenly needed the man naked and between my legs. I glanced at him and he caught my eye. The adoration I saw in his expression was too much for me to process, so I shut down, dropping my eyes to my iPad for a moment to gather my thoughts.

Shit! Shit! Shit! I was falling for this man. I needed to cut it off at the knees, but I didn't know how I'd do that, considering he was expecting me in his bed tonight.

Why did I agree to this? I was an idiot.

Taking a deep breath, I focused back on Jack again, who was back to being engulfed in his music and tried to separate my heart from my vagina.

* * *

Jack

There are only two things in life I can compare to playing live music; sex and riding a horse. In all three activities, there is a balancing act between being in complete control, and surrendering to the random chaos around you. Moments of fear being overtaken by feelings of rapture. Potential glories and failures battling it out in the pit of your stomach. I'd long since replaced, or at least attempted to replace, drumming with other adrenaline raising activities, but now that I'd found myself here again, I knew I was right where I was supposed to be.

"We've got a few more songs for you, if that's alright." Rex's voice echoed throughout the venue. The crowd roared back in approval and I readied myself for Robbie to start the next song.

"Before we do that, I'd like to thank my brothers for being up here with me tonight. I can't tell you how much it means to me to be playing with these two guys again."

In all the countless shows we'd played over the years,

I'd never recalled Rex introducing us on stage, or anything like that. We'd come up during a time when such things felt like "rock star" moves. However, this felt different, and I fought my nature to withdraw when I felt too much attention on me.

"Ladies and gentlemen, please show your love to Mr. Robbie Roberts on the guitar!" Rex shouted, and the place responded in kind. Rex continued. "I know a lot of you have travelled a long way to be here with us, but I assure you, nobody has come further in order to be here tonight than the man behind the drums. Please let him know how much you've missed him...Jack Henry."

The applause that followed was like nothing I'd ever experienced. The cheers were nearly deafening, and seemed to increase over the following minutes. I knew our music had been really important to a lot of young people in the 90's, but I had no idea how much I figured into that. I don't tend to dwell on the past, but rather draw my energy from the possible future.

"From me, Jack and Robbie, I just want to say thank you and we love you!" Rex yelled and Robbie ripped into the opening riff of "Box of Matches."

As we played through our final song of the set, I found myself looking to the side of the stage more and more often. I'd tried my best to shut Hadley out of my mind while we were playing, and had been pretty successful for most of the night. However, this was opening night and my brain was plenty occupied. As of now, the countdown clock to when I'd have Hadley in my bed started ticking and it was getting harder to think of much else.

We finished the tune and exited the stage the second it went dark. The video screens came to life again, which meant we had three minutes before our encore. I searched for Hadley in the low light, but couldn't see her anywhere. "You were amazing." I felt her breath as she whispered into my ear. She had snuck up behind me in the darkness and I could feel her hand slip into mine. "You just wait until later," I whispered back, still unable to see her. She squeezed my hand, and before I could turn around, had slipped back into the darkness.

Every drummer will tell you that a sudden surge of adrenaline will cause you to rush the tempo while playing. If anyone should wonder why I played our final song that night way too fast, they could blame Hadley Simon.

* * *

Hadley

After Jack's performance, my body was locked and loaded for some of his magic. I should probably be more specific…my vagina was locked and loaded for some of his magic. Actually, my vagina was always locked and loaded when it came to Jack Henry and his level fifty-seven wizardry of the cock.

Lucy and I were currently at the hotel, gathering everyone's keys, and making sure rooms were on the right floors. I was lingering, hoping Lucy would walk away for just a few minutes, so I could…

"Oh, crap, Mom's calling," Lucy said. "You good?"

"I'm great," I said, and she walked away.

I faced the front desk person and said, "I need two rooms with adjoining doors, please."

"We have two on the executive level, but you have only reserved one."

"It's all good, can we add that, please?"

"Sure thing. Your total will be increased by four-hundred-sixty-seven dollars and seventy-two cents."

I tried not to choke. That would put a big hit in my bank

account. "No problem. Can you put that one on my personal credit card, please?"

"Sure thing."

I handed it over with a grimace and the woman ran it through. I slid the card into my pocket and then gathered the rest, jotting down the card key numbers with the assigned band member, roadie, or other.

Lucy returned just as the rest of the folks filed in. She and I took care of everyone, giving them all their pertinent details and handing out an updated schedule.

We had a break day before heading out on Sunday morning for California, so we'd hired a boat to take anyone who wanted to go out on the Columbia, but tonight, I had Jack all to myself and I needed it...needed *him*.

Once everyone had dispersed and I was left with Lucy in the lobby, I told her I was going to grab a few things from the little gift shop before heading to my room. I didn't want her to know I wasn't sleeping on her floor tonight, but couldn't think of another way to "lose" her.

As I headed back through the lobby, I felt a bit like I was in a James Bond movie, circumventing open spaces, opting to walk behind large pieces of furniture and potted plants (cartoon piano sounds under my footsteps included in my imaginary soundtrack). I stepped into the elevator and headed to my floor, peeking into the hallway and checking it was clear before making a run for my room.

I let myself in and then leaned against the door to catch my breath. Pulling out my cell phone, I texted Jack and then walked into my very expensive, tap into my savings account, there goes the extra night in Paris fund, room.

I heard a quiet knock at the adjoining door, so I pulled it open and found myself lifted off the ground and kissed for everything I was worth.

"Fuck me, I've missed you," Jack said, dropping me on the bed.

I giggled. "You just saw me an hour ago."

"Too long," he growled and hovered over me.

I stroked his beard and smiled. "You were *amazing* tonight. Amazing. One day, I'd like you to teach me that fill you do coming out of the chorus on Stephen's Song."

"One day, I wanna hear you play."

"Deal."

He kissed me again, then stretched out beside me, waving his hand around the room. "This gonna be a regular thing?"

"Adjoining rooms?"

I nodded. "If they have them and they don't cost what they cost tonight, sure."

"What do you mean? We're payin' for it."

"Um, no, you're not, Jack. I'm not charging RatHound for me to upgrade to an executive level room because I don't want anyone to know I have a fuck-buddy on this trip."

He chuckled. "Fuck-buddy, huh?"

I grinned. "You wanna get to that, *buddy?*"

He climbed off the bed and removed his clothing and I followed suit. I sat on the edge of the mattress and pulled him closer to me where I wrapped my fingers around his hardening length and slid my hand down, cupping him before taking his cock into my mouth.

Jack hissed, fisting his hands in my hair, but before I could get to anything fun, I lost purchase on his dick and I was dragged up his body. "Hey!" I snapped.

"On your knees."

I wanted to complain about not getting the chance to finish what I started, but on my knees was my one of my favorite positions, so I kept my mouth shut and did as I was told. Jack guided himself inside of me and I dropped my head back at the sensation.

"You like this, Hadley?" he asked as his palm connected

with my ass.

I whimpered and pushed my body back against him.

"Mmm, you like that, huh?" He slammed into me again, his palm slapping me a little harder this time and the sensation overtook everything. God, it felt amazing, but when he slid one hand between my legs and fingered my clit, I came the second the palm of his other hand slapped against my bottom again, and I cried out his name as I buried my face in the mattress while he continued to thrust into me. His body locked and he wrapped his arms around me, gently rolling us to the side so we were spooning, staying connected as he kissed the back of my neck. "I think we need to get out of the fuck-buddy zone."

I grinned as I tried to catch my breath. "You want to level up?"

He kissed my shoulder. "Yeah, baby, whatever the fuck that means."

"It's a gaming term."

"Gaming term?"

"Video games, you know?"

"Holy shit, you're a geek!" he exclaimed.

I laughed. "Guilty."

"Well, don't tell anyone...you were one of the kids who got shoved into lockers at my high school."

I shifted so I was straddling him and leaned down to kiss him. "No one *ever* shoved me in a locker."

He gripped my hips, lifting me slightly, then lowering me onto his already hard cock. I let out a quiet moan and he grinned as he sat up and kissed me. "No, can't imagine they would."

I lifted myself and then lowered slowly. "Of course, if you'd been the one shoving..."

He buried his face in my neck. "Yeah, baby, gonna do some shovin'."

For the next blissful hour or two, Jack and I explored

each other until I could no longer keep my eyes open. I hadn't realized just how tired I was until I was snuggled up against his glorious body.

"You don't have to be there tomorrow, right?" Jack asked.

"Um, yes I actually do."

"It's optional."

"It's optional for *you* guys, but since Lucy and I organized it, it's important for us to both be there." I leaned over him so I could meet his eyes. "Besides, I want to see the river and some of the city. I've never seen the west coast, and I plan to take advantage of all of it."

"So I guess I'm gettin' on a boat tomorrow."

I stroked his cheek. "I promise I'll find a place we can make out a little."

He chuckled. "I'll hold you to that."

Jack

TOUR BUSSES ARE an interesting, and very specific microcosm. They are equal parts hotel room, airplane cabin, locker room, and insane asylum. To travel in one for any amount of time requires a great deal of tolerance and understanding. If patience is not a virtue one possesses, then it helps to be certifiably insane, or out of your tree on drugs and alcohol. Since this tour was dry as a nun's gusset, and I was by far *not* the world's most patient man, I knew I was in for a bit of a rough haul.

"We've come a long way since Sally, haven't we?" Rex asked. We stood facing our current home, a 2012 Barracuda touring coach, which was indeed a far sight better ride than our first band van.

"Yeah, but Sally had a better rear end."

"You always were an ass man weren't you, Jack?" Rex smiled. "You ready to get back on board this pirate ship?" I gave him a salute. "Aye, aye, cap'n." I looked around for Hadley, but couldn't spot her. We'd had a perfect day out on the water yesterday, and I'd had her in my bed for two nights in a row, so now that we were apart, I was missing her again. She was likely already on her bus, trying not to draw any attention to us, and as much as I wanted to see her, I was starting to share in her feeling that suspicious eyes were on us. In fact, two of those eyes were currently walking toward us.

"Good morning Daddy, Uncle Jack," Lucy said, looking like she was ready to take on the world. Last night's opening show was a huge success, and that was a major win for our new manager. We had done great business for ourselves and the venue, and more importantly, we showed the world that RatHound was back in full force.

"Hey, baby girl. Did you get enough rest last night?" Rex asked, kissing her cheek.

"Barely. I was so wired after the show. You guys were seriously amazing. I couldn't be prouder of you. This tour is going to be better than I'd even hoped."

Even though she looked a little tired, Lucy was beaming. I could tell she wasn't just happy for us, but that she was truly happy with her life. She had obviously found something special with Bam, as well as her true calling as a manager, and I was thrilled to see her so content, and in her element. For the first time, I felt a pang for not being around more when she was growing up. It was hard for me to see my friends with their young families, when I never really got to start mine. I resolved to use this tour as an opportunity to spend more time with my niece, and tried to convince myself it wasn't partly in an effort to spend more time publicly with Hadley.

"You looking for someone, Uncle Jack?" Lucy asked.

"Huh? No. Why?"

"Oh, it just looks like your eyes are peeled...like you're lookin' for someone."

"Nope. I'm just taking it all in, ya know? It's been a while since I've lived on a bus. This will be my first overnighter in a while."

"Oh, okay." She smiled just as her phone rang.

Saved by the bell.

Lucy answered. "Hey, Mama, what's up? What? When? Is anything missing? What did Vic say? Yeah, he's here. Do you want to talk to him?" She handed the phone to Rex.

"What's going on? Is everything okay?" I asked.

"Someone broke into the studio," Lucy said.

"Into Fastback? When?"

"The night before we left."

I felt my face heat up. That was the night Hadley and I snuck in after hours and fucked on the lobby sofa. I don't know why I was worried. It's not like anyone could know it was us who had "broken in." There must have been a time entry in the alarm system's log that stuck out to Vic and his eye for detail.

"They didn't appear to steal anything, which means they were either some stalker level RatHound fans, or they got spooked off before they could steal anything."

"Spooked off? By what, the studio attack dogs?" I tried laughing it off.

"I don't know, maybe they saw the cameras or something."

"Cameras?" The blood that had rushed to my head, now completely drained and I felt instantly sick. "Yeah, luckily the studio has surveillance cameras all around the studio. I doubt they would have spotted them, though, they're pretty concealed."

Tell me about it.

Rex hung up and joined us. "Roxie has asked Vic to review the footage and email Lucy the video file right away. She doesn't want to file a police report if it ends up being nothing. No sense in alerting the insurance company vampires if we don't have to."

This is it. Vic is going to watch the tapes, tell Lucy, Roxie, and Rex what he saw and this will have been the shortest tour in rock and roll history. At least they aren't going to call the cops yet.

Just then, I spotted Hadley walking toward the Roses for Anna bus.

"Alright, I'm gonna go get on board, I'll see you two on the bus," I said and began walking briskly. When I was almost at our bus, I checked over my shoulder to make sure I wasn't being watched by Rex and Lucy, and cut over to Hadley's bus. I hung near the back and texted for her to come outside.

"Hey, what are you doing here?" she asked in a sexy whisper.

"We have a little problem. Actually, we have a big problem."

Hadley stopped smiling and my heart sunk. "What kind of problem?" Her eyes were now set directly on me in a steely gaze.

"The kind of problem where there's security video of us having sex in the studio lobby."

"*WHAT?*"

"Shhhhh," I hissed. "That's not all."

"Ohmigod, it gets worse?"

"Rex, Roxie, and Lucy are about to see it."

* * *

Hadley

"I think I'm gonna throw up."

"Just breathe, baby," Jack said, in a soothing tone. "Shut your stupid face, and don't call me baby," I whisper-yelled. The hotel coffee was not nearly strong enough for this level of fuckery so early in the day, and he was not going to charm his way out of this one.

"Babe, it's—"

"Wait, I really think I am gonna throw up." Luckily, I had walked past the piles of bacon, eggs and cinnamon rolls at this morning's breakfast buffet, instead opting for my usual yogurt and granola. I say fortunately, because that's all Jack had to clean off his snakeskin boots after I hurled directly on them.

"Ohmigod, Jack, I'm so sorry," I cried, mortified at what I'd just done.

"I deserved that," Jack said.

Holy shit, the man was charming even when I was puking on him.

"Here." Jack pulled a blue bandana from his inside pocket and handed it to me.

I bent down to clean the mess from his boots, but he grabbed my arm and laughed.

"What are you doing, you lunatic?" he demanded. "That's for your beautiful face, not my boots."

"Omigod I think I'm in shock. This can't be happening. There can't be a sex tape. There can't be a sex tape. Jack, there absolutely can*not* be a sex tape."

"Look, I get it, this is bad and super embarrassing, but we're adults and—"

"No, I don't think you do get it." I snapped, still obsessively wiping my face.

"You...uh...missed a spot," Jack said, grinning.

"This is not funny. You've practically lived off the grid for the past century, so you don't know what Bam has gone through."

"What?"

"Do you know who Melody Morgan is?" I asked.

"Rex mentioned her once I think. She's a singer, right?"

"Yes, a very popular pop singer. She's beautiful...on the outside at least...and she and Bam used to date. They had a very public relationship, followed by a very public breakup, in which a sex tape was involved."

"Oh, shit!"

"Oh, shit indeed," I ground out. "If Lucy, Bam, or the Haddon family see that tape, I'm not only fired, they're going to hate me!"

"Hate you? Why in the word would they hate you? You haven't done anything wrong."

"Except make web cam porn with my employer, after hours at the workplace, after their family had already endured a humiliating sex scandal," I hissed.

"Well, when you put it that way," he smiled wide.

"Jack, it's not funny. I—"

"Wait a minute! Maybe I can get ahold of Vic and somehow head them off at the pass," Jack said, pulling out his cell phone.

"What are you going to say to him?"

"I dunno, I'll think on my feet. Pretty sure I can handle a little mental sparing with Vic."

After a few tense moments, Vic answered and I leaned close to Jack's phone.

"Hey Jack, I figured you'd be calling," Vic answered in his usual monotone drone. "I found the footage of the intruders and figured you'd want to identify the perps before the others saw this. I've isolated the pertinent video files, and stored the only copies on a thumb drive, which will remain locked in my safe until you retrieve it. I'll let Lucy know about the false alarm and that I've fixed the glitch in the security software. I'll also text you the address where you can send the four leather tour jackets, full access passes to the Seattle show, and go ahead and chuck in a few Roses for Anna T-Shirts as well. Thanks."

We stood in stunned silence unable to determine whether we should laugh or cry.

"I should get back on the bus," I finally said.

"Yeah, uh, me too. After I clean the puke off my boots...and die of a heart attack."

I took several deep breaths, trying not to hyperventilate as I walked back to the bus. God! Today had started out so beautifully. I'd come downstairs to check everyone out, discovered Jack had paid for my room (one more night in Paris was back on the table), and even managed to get a discount for a future stay. I felt like I was rockin' my job and my life and felt like a million bucks.

Funny how the potential scandal of a sexual escapade could bring all of that crashing down.

* * *

Jack

That was way too close. Apparently Big Brother didn't even have to be forced upon us. We'd installed it ourselves in the name of security. Now an enterprising engineer (that's on my payroll) can blackmail me for fucking on the couch.

I dragged my hands down my face. We were actually damn lucky Vic was doing us a solid by protecting me and Hadley's privacy. His way of doing it showed ultra class, in that it allowed me to save face and avoid dancing around the subject with him. I'd always appreciated his directness, but now I realized it was invaluable.

"Whose turn is it to DJ?" Robbie shouted. Robbie had always served as the band's "Cruise Director" while on tour, earning him the nickname Julie. Julie would serve drinks, make introductions, plan late night mayhem, and was largely responsible for most of the hotel damage we'd paid for over the years. "I'll take first shift." I needed a distraction from this morning's events and music seemed like just the trick. I rifled through several binders of CDs and chose an album from the criminally underrated King's X. I knew the entire bus would be onboard and that the volume would be cranked the entire time. I could avoid talking to anyone and get lost in my thoughts. As the opening of "Dogman" slammed through the bus's sound system, its passengers collectively grunted and nodded in approval. We had the great fortune to tour with King's X in the 90's and could never understand why they weren't the biggest band on the planet. In fact, almost every musician or music lover I knew felt the exact same way.

My phone buzzed. It was a text from Hadley.

We need to talk

So much for relaxing and getting lost in my thoughts. I may not be the wisest man in the world, but I'd been around long enough to know it's never a good thing when a woman says we need to talk.

About what? I replied.

You know about what. That was way too close this morning. We have to stop sneaking around.

Are you suggesting we go public?

No. Let's talk face-to-face when we stop next.

If you want to talk about how to be more careful, I'm all ears. If you want to talk about ending things between us, I'm afraid I'm not available for such a meeting.

I'm serious. We can't keep doing this. People are going

to get hurt.

I frowned. *By people you mean you?*

That's not fair, Jack. This isn't just about me, or even you. Both of our bands are entwined in all this mess as well.

Are you saying you and I are a mess?

Jack, there isn't even a "you and I."

Ouch. *Look, I know that you and I joke around about being fuck buddies, but I hope you know that's not how I feel about you.*

I can't talk about this right now. We'll meet face-to-face as soon as possible.

With that, my phone went silent. I also barely made a sound for the next four hours. I sat there trying to figure out how to convince Hadley to continue to risk her career, along with relationships with her family and best friend, in order to continue our secret screw fest. I knew she was right, but that didn't matter. There was no way I could let Hadley go. No way in hell.

We pulled into a Denny's in Grants Pass, Oregon for lunch. Across the street was a giant statue of the "Grants Pass Caveman," and all the band and crew members from each bus were gathering around for a group photo. I tried to position myself next to Hadley, but she moved to the other side of the group and stood between Bam and his drum tech, Ray. She refused to make eye contact with me and casually avoided me as our group made its way into the restaurant.

"We need as many tables and booths as you can spare, please," Lucy cheerfully informed Jeff, the day manager.

I saw Ray grab a booth in the far corner and motion to Hadley. She sat next to him and my blood began to boil. I was sitting with Rex, Roxie, and Lucy at a four-seat table across the room. My eyes were fixed on Hadley, or more specifically at her and the dead-man-walking sitting next to her.

"And for you, sir?" our waiter asked, bringing my focus back to the table.

"Coffee, black, thanks."

"You're a man of many words today, Uncle Jack," Lucy teased.

"Yeah, probably just a bit tired after last night," I said.

"Didn't you sleep well?"

"I was a little wired, so not so much."

I glanced back at Hadley, who was now laughing hysterically at something that little roadie cheese dick was saying to her. What the fuck did this little weasel think he was doing? Hadley's Roses' manager and he's the band's drum tech. She was out of his league, and reach, in every possible way but he's clearly coming on hard and she didn't appear to be stopping him.

She laughed again, and I saw Ray's hand touch hers. I stood straight up. "If you guys will excuse me, I'm gonna go wash my hands," I said, and started walking towards Hadley's table.

Hadley caught my eye and stood, heading to the bathroom.

"Hey, Jack," Ray said, stopping me in my tracks.

"Hey, man."

"Great show."

"Thanks."

Ray grinned. "I gotta talk to Teddy and find out how he gets that beefy snare drum sound on Stephen's Song."

"It's called tuning," I ground out. "Excuse me, yeah? Gotta hit the head."

"Oh, yeah. Sure."

I walked toward the bathrooms and arrived just as Hadley walked out of the ladies.

"Anyone in there?" I asked.

"No."

I pushed her gently back inside and up against the wall,

kissing her for all she was worth. She gripped my waist and kissed me back.

"This is all gonna be okay, Hadley," I whispered.

She sagged against me. "We need to be more careful."

"And we will." I pulled her closer. "Vic took care of the video problem and we'll just make sure we are a little more covert."

She nodded. "Okay."

"Like this, baby."

She smiled. "Me too."

"Your stomach feelin' better?"

"Much. I ate some saltines on the bus."

I stroked her cheek. "Good. I'm gonna miss you tonight."

"Me too." She sighed. "And I don't think the hotel in Ashland has adjoining rooms."

"I'll come to you. You just tell me where and I'll figure out when."

She smiled, dropping her head to my chest. "Okay, honey."

"You need to stay away from Ray."

"I'm finding that harder and harder to do."

"You need me to take care of it?"

"No, I'll do it." She met my eyes. "I should get back out there."

"One more second."

She grinned and kissed me again, and then stepped into the hallway, gave me the all-clear, and I walked into the men's room.

* * *

Hadley

I headed back out into the dining room, and rushed past the table Ray was currently sitting at with a few of the other roadies. His back was to me, so he didn't see me coming,

121

which meant I made it to Bam and Lucy's table without incident.

I sat down and had just enough time to look the menu over before the waitress arrived to take our order.

Jack walked by a few seconds later and I gave him a quick smile, hoping that everything I felt was said in my slight facial expression. He stopped and talked with us for a few minutes, then headed back to his table, but I didn't miss his hand brushing my arm gently as he passed.

I couldn't wait for tomorrow night when I'd sleep beside him again. It really couldn't come soon enough.

CHAPTER THIRTEEN

Hadley

WE'D MADE IT to Ashland early, so several of the crew had decided to head into town to explore. I was exhausted, so I chose to stay back at my room, but a knock at my door had me groaning in frustration as I turned off the taps of the bath I was about to enjoy.

I peeked through the peephole and yanked the door open. "What are you doing here?"

Jack chuckled and walked inside, closing and locking the door behind us. "Found out you weren't goin' anywhere, so I found an excuse to do the same."

I grinned, leaning up to kiss him. "Sounds delicious, but you're interrupting my bath plans."

"How about I get you dirty and then you can soak while I order room service."

I shivered. "I love that idea."

He kissed me again, lifting my T-shirt off my body and guiding me to the bed, pushing me gently onto the mattress and dragging my pants down... panties and all... and throwing them aside. He climbed up my body, kissing as he went, pushing my bra off as he moved up. I arched as he drew a nipple into his mouth and slid a hand between my legs, thumbing my clit.

"Jack," I breathed out.

"Open, baby."

I dropped my knees so he could have better access and he slid three fingers inside of me, gently biting down on my nipple. I mewed, my breath coming in pants as he sped up his hand between my legs. "Ohmigod, *yes*."

His hand slipped out of me and I whimpered, but I needn't have been concerned, because his mouth replaced his thumb and his fingers slid back inside of me. I cried out as my orgasm hit and my legs became like jelly

Jack kissed me gently and pushed off the bed. He removed his clothes and even in my climax-induced haze, I was transfixed by his body. He might have been a decade older than me, but you'd never know it. He was gorgeous and his body was like granite. He was hard and his cock was just as impressive as his body. I licked my lips, suddenly wanting him in my mouth. I sat up and scooted off the bed, kneeling in front of him.

"Baby, wait."

I shook my head, cradling his cock in my hand and kissing the tip. I took as much of him as I could in my mouth. God, he was big...deliciously so.

"Hadley," he whispered.

I released him and frowned up at him. "Would you please stop talking, Jack?"

I slid my mouth over the tip again and drew him further in.

"Condom," he whispered.

I groaned and continued to suck as I pumped with one hand and cradled his balls with the other.

I knew I was giving him what he needed when he fisted his hands into my hair and his hips began to move. I couldn't stop a smile as he fucked my mouth, me a willing participant, holding on when he told me he was going to come. He warned me again, but I grabbed his ass and squeezed.

"Holy shit!" he said with a groan as he came.

I waited until his cock stopped pulsing before giving one more suck and releasing him. Jack moved quickly as he lifted and dropped me back on the bed, sliding into me slowly (after putting on a condom), but no less deliciously.

"Honey," I whispered.

He kissed me and his tongue swept against mine as he surged into me. Guiding my hands above my head, Jack held them there with one hand, sliding his other to my breast. As he rolled my nipple between his fingers, he kissed me deeply, slamming into me over and over again.

I cried out his name as I came, trying to drag my hands from their prison to touch him, but he held firm and didn't release me until he came inside of me, eliciting yet another orgasm from me.

He kissed me again and pulled me close, running his fingers through my hair. "Gorgeous, baby."

I ran my finger down his chest. "This all gets better and better."

"Yeah, it does."

"But that bath beckons, so I'm going to put in the room service order and you can wait for it." I sat up and grabbed the menu. "What do you want?"

"I can do it, baby."

"No, I don't want a man calling down from my room."

"What about opening the door to receive it?" he challenged.

"Since you'll be fully clothed, we can explain that away."

He chuckled. "You'd be a good spy."

"Thank you." I ordered our food and then went back to the bathroom and added hot water before sliding into the warmth.

Soft whiskers settled on my forehead and Jack kissed me there and I opened my eyes with a smile. "Is the food here?"

"Yeah."

"That was quick."

"Not really. You fell asleep. It took forty-five minutes."

"Seriously?" I sat up. "I must be getting too old for tour life."

Jack laughed. "I hear ya."

"You better not keep me up all night, mister." I jabbed a finger toward him. "I need to sleep."

He laughed, grabbing my hand and lifting me out of the tub before handing me a towel. "I'll see what I can do."

I pulled on a robe and joined Jack back in the room where we ate, then spent the evening watching television and fucking like rabbits, but he was forever a gentleman, so he made sure we were tucked into bed by nine and I fell asleep soon after, snuggled close to the man who was rapidly wrapping himself around my heart.

* * *

We hit California and I couldn't wait to explore San Francisco. Roxie had organized a girls' night out, so the three of us were going to dinner then dancing...no boys allowed.

The show at the Oracle Arena was on Saturday night, but tonight, we were letting our hair down, and after being surrounded by testosterone for a couple of weeks, I was ready for some lady time.

I'd brought a little black dress with me (well, actually, it was red) and a pair of strappy heeled sandals, but the night was chilly and overcast, so I quickly wished I had a nicer pair of shoes. I didn't travel with much on the road, so my only "evening" shoes were the sandals.

I had lamented as much to Jack in bed last night as I was perusing the Zon trying to find something I could have delivered to me at the hotel. Alas, everything I liked was either way out of my budget, or not available for same-day delivery.

I was going to freeze.

A knock at my door brought Jack and I yanked him into the room with a frown. "What are you doing here?" I hissed. "Someone will see you."

He chuckled. "Baby, no one's even walkin' around on this floor. I checked."

Unfortunately, the hotel's adjoining rooms were all booked, so we were stuck on separate floors. He pulled a bag out from behind his back with a huge smile.

"What's this?"

"A gift. Open it."

I bit my lip and peeked in the bag. "Ohmigod. No." I glanced up at him and back in the bag, dragging the shoe box out of it. "You did not."

They were the Louboutin black suede booties I'd been drooling over before checking out Payless Shoes for a cheaper version. The red sole matched my dress perfectly and I found myself stroking them before shoving them back in the box. "I can't."

"Why the hell not?"

"They're, like, almost a grand. No. Huh-uh. I can't."

"Sit down, Hadley."

"Jack—"

"Sit down," he growled, and I sat.

He took the boots out of the box again and slid them gently onto my feet and I groaned as he pulled me back up. "They feel like butter."

He chuckled. "They look perfect, baby."

"Well, they better for what they cost."

"What are you wearing?"

I nodded to the dress hanging over the door. "That."

"Ah, no you're not."

"Why not?"

"That'll barely cover your ass."

I rolled my eyes. "It's not *that* skimpy."

"Baby, no."

"Ohmigod, Jack, you don't get to dictate what I wear."

He dropped his head back and swore before dragging his hands down his face and staring at me intently.

"Jack?"

"Workin' it out, baby. Give me a second."

I grabbed the dress off the hanger, slid my robe from my shoulders, and stepped into the fabric. "Zip me."

Jack stepped toward me, and zipped it up, kissing the back of my neck before he did the final hook at the top.

"You work it out yet?" I asked, and turned to face him again.

"No," he breathed out. "Fuck. Baby, you seriously goin' out like that?"

The dress was low-cut and fitted with a rouched panel over the waist and stopped just above the knee. It looked great on my curves and had a little stretch in it, so I didn't walk like a Geisha.

"You don't like it?"

"The problem is, I like it a fuck of a lot...and so will every dick that'll be following you."

I chuckled. "You're ridiculous."

"I don't like that you're goin' out without someone watchin' your back."

"Sully will be there."

"He's one guy to the three of you, and he's paid to watch Lucy, so she'll get first bullet."

"Wait a minute." I laid my palm on his chest. "I thought I was just supposed to be worried about barflies, now people are shooting at us?"

"Metaphorically. If someone's hittin' on you and Lucy, who do you think Sully's gonna stop first?"

I grabbed my earrings and put them on with a smile. "You're forgetting Roxie."

"Roxie can take care of herself. I've seen her take down a man twice my size in ten-point-two seconds."

"And you don't think I can?"

"Not in that dress, no."

I tapped my lip with my finger and mused out loud, "Do I burst his bubble now or never?"

He crossed his arms. "If you say you can take care of yourself, I believe you, Hadley, but if some asshole puts something in your drink, you won't be lucid enough to fight him off."

I pulled his arms away from his chest and wrapped mine around his waist. "I won't drink anything I don't get directly from a server or the bartender and I will drink mostly bottled water...that I open myself." I cocked my head. "Are you okay if I drink? Because I won't if it'll bother you."

"Knock yourself out, baby, just be smart."

"Are you sure?"

"Yeah. You've been dry for weeks. Have a little fun."

"Thanks, honey. I will. I will also make sure bathroom visits are executed with my bathroom buddy...or Sully... although, he might get sick of watching us go in and out of the ladies'."

"I think we should go with you."

"No!" I gave him a gentle squeeze. "It's our time away from the farting, ball scratching, and general grossness of you men and I plan to take advantage of that."

"I don't fart, nor do I scratch my balls in public, so that means you just find me gross."

"Not even a little bit." I giggled. "The others, though...well, they're not you, and I want to have some girl time."

He sighed, leaning down to kiss me. "You look beautiful."

"You could have opened with that, but the shoes were a good buffer."

He smiled...finally and kissed me again. "I kind of want you out of that dress now."

"Later," I promised. "Right now, I need to see the whole ensemble."

He released me and I walked into the bathroom where there was a full-length mirror, and did a little happy dance.

"Good?"

I squeaked and threw my arms around his neck. "They're amazing, honey. Thank you, thank you, thank you."

"You could have led with that instead of shoving them back in the box," he retorted.

I sighed. "I know. I'm sorry. I'm not used to being spoiled, and this was a huge gift, Jack. I still feel weird taking it."

"Do they make you happy?"

"*You* make me happy."

He grinned. "Good answer."

I kissed him gently. "Thank you. They are exactly what I wanted and they look perfect with this dress."

"When you get back, you're gonna remove the dress, but keep those boots on."

I licked my lips. "Okay, honey, I can get behind that."

A knock sounded and I gasped. "Who is that?"

"Probably Lucy."

"She can't see you in here!" I hissed and pushed him toward the bathroom. "Hide."

"What if she has to take a piss?"

"I'll tell her...ah...I'll tell her I just took a giant dump and she should wait until we get to the lobby."

He chuckled. "You've obviously been around the boys a lot longer than you're willing to admit."

"Hence the girls' night. Now, hide," I said, pushing him harder toward the bathroom. "There's a key on the dresser for you to use later."

Jack closed himself into the bathroom and I grabbed my purse and coat and headed to the door. It was in fact Lucy, so I stepped out of the room with a grin. "Ohmigod, I'm so excited."

She grinned. "You look amazing."

"Thank you, so do you."

Lucy wore a stunning black dress that had a crisscross top with wide shoulder straps, and a loose skirt that fell just above her knees. She wore a pair of heels that had a bow around her ankle and she looked sexy and sweet all at the same time.

"Where's your mom?"

"She's currently in a rip-roaring argument with my dad who has decreed, 'you will not go out alone in that,'" Lucy mimicked.

Hmmm, Rex and Jack were apparently cut from the same cloth.

I giggled. "Let's go save her, then."

We headed upstairs to the executive suites, and Lucy knocked on the door, entering when Roxie pulled the door open.

"Holy crap, Mom, you look amazing," Lucy exclaimed

and hugged her.

"Thanks, baby, so do you."

Roxie wore a lace dress that had a black under dress, and it fell to just below her knees. She was a fuller figured woman and it complemented all of her curves perfectly. She'd teased her blonde hair and layered on the smoky eye, but kept her lips and cheeks somewhat neutral. If I didn't know she was in her fifties, I would have sworn she was my age.

"You really do look amazing," I said, and Roxie grinned.

"You do too, honey. I think we're gonna find you a man tonight."

I choked a little and forced a smile. "Nope. Not interested in finding a man, but thanks."

"Well, maybe just a one-night stand."

"Roxanne MacDonald Haddon, there will be no pickin' men up…for anyone," Rex bellowed from the other room, and I couldn't stop a laugh as he walked out of the bedroom with a scowl. "Hear me?"

"Yeah, baby, the whole hotel heard you," she retorted, and wrapped her arms around his waist. "I love you, you big dope."

"Love you too, baby." His hands went straight to her ass and he squeezed.

I turned away from the slightly erotic scene and busied myself in my purse, grabbing my lipstick and running it lightly over my mouth.

"Really, you two?" Lucy complained, and Rex chuckled.

"You know the drill, baby girl."

"Yeah, I know. Mom's ass is always at your disposal, privately or otherwise. Gross."

I blushed, but stayed silent. I thought it was sweet. They'd been together for thirty years or something close to that, and they were still madly in love with each other.

Lucy glanced at her phone. "Sully's in the hallway."

"We better go, then," Roxie said, and leaned up to kiss Rex. "Be good."

"You too."

She grinned. "No way in hell."

We laughed and rushed out of the room before he could stop us.

"Ladies," Sully said, and waved toward the elevators.

I looped my arm with Lucy's and we were practically giddy as we headed down the hall...just as Jack turned the corner.

"You're gonna be givin' the bouncers a workout tonight," Jack said with a grin.

"We're gonna be giving the bartenders a workout tonight," Roxie quipped.

I bit my lip as Jack's eyes raked over my body and I couldn't help a little shiver.

"You ladies have a good time. I'll keep Rex and Bam occupied."

"Thanks, Uncle Jack," Lucy said, and we continued to the elevator.

* * *

Arriving back at the hotel, Bam and Rex had met Roxie and Lucy in the parking garage in order to walk them to their rooms, so Sully walked me to mine. I was somewhat intoxicated and found this funny for some reason.

"You really are the Sullynator," I quipped as we rode the elevator up.

"The Sullynator, Miss Simon?"

"You know, like the Terminator...only Sully. Sullynator." I giggled. "It just rolls off your tongue."

The doors popped open and I stumbled out, laughing again when Sully wrapped an arm around my waist and tugged me the opposite way. "This way, Miss Simon."

"Are you sure?"

"Yes."

"You're should really say, 'Come with me if you want to live,'" I said in my best Arnold voice.

His lips went up...sort of.

"Did I just make you smile?" I squeaked. "Did I just make the Sullynator smile?"

"We're here, Miss Simon," he said, his mouth now back to his normal bodyguard expression. "Do you have your key?"

"My key?"

"Your room key."

"Oh, right." I grabbed my purse and rummaged in it, finding the key and waving it triumphantly in the air. "I found it!"

"Well, done, Miss Simon. Can I help you open your door?"

I giggled. "Are you flirting with me, Mr. Sullivan?"

"Just trying to make sure you get in your room safely."

"Do you have a lady friend, Sully?" I continued, my filter totally clocked with the alcohol coursing through my veins.

"No, ma'am."

"That can't be right, because you're super handsome, Sully. You look like young Pierce Brosnan. Come to think of it, old Pierce Brosnan looks like young Pierce Brosnan. I'm not actually sure he's aging. Do you think anyone's ever actually looked into that, Sully?

"No, ma'am."

"They should. And this all begs the question, why don't you have a lady friend? You should have a lady friend. You're too handsome not to have a lady friend." I gasped. "Do you want a gentleman friend instead, Sully? I should probably stop talking about the *ladies* if you'd rather have a gentleman friend."

"No, ma'am."

"Oh, then you really *should* have a lady friend. Do you need help finding a lady friend? I bet Lucy and I could find you a lady friend." I giggled. "Lady friend is such a funny word to say...well, it's really two words, but they're funny, don't you think, Sully...nator?"

"Yes, ma'am, they're funny." He gently pried my room key from my hand and unlocked my door, handing it back to me as he pushed the door open slightly. "In you go."

"Okay. Right. Thanks, Sully."

"Hasta la vista, Miss Simon."

I exploded into giggles as I stepped into my room and Sully pulled the door closed behind me.

"Fuck me, baby, I thought I was gonna have to come out there and collect you."

I squealed in fright, flipping on the light. "What are you doing here?"

"You gave me a key." He chuckled. "Didn't mean to scare you."

I wrinkled my nose. "I didn't think you'd be here waiting for me."

"You'd rather it be Sully?"

"What? No!" I frowned. "What?"

Jack chuckled. "Okay, baby, you need to get out of that dress and sleep."

"But I wanted to keep my boots on while you...did stuff to me." I licked my lips, but found myself really interested in the flavor of the lip-gloss I was wearing. "Ohmigod, my lips taste like lollipops."

Jack grinned. "I'm sure they do. Come on...I'll help you with your boots."

"You should really lick my lips and then you'll taste the lollipop too."

"I'll lick them later...when I do stuff to you."

"Why not now?"

"Because you're drunk, and as gorgeous and adorable as you are, I want you a little more sober before I lick...well, everything."

"You're always such a gentleman," I said, hiccupping as I leaned against him. "Why am I hiccupping?"

"Because you're drunk."

"I thought hiccupping only happened in cartoons."

He chuckled. "Well, apparently, you just proved that theory wrong."

I smiled up at him. "You are so unbelievably delicious."

"Thank you, baby."

"Can I taste *your* lollipop?"

He groaned, dropping his head back. "I'm holdin' on by a thread here, Hadley."

I grinned, kissing his neck, and then I think I passed out.

* * *

Jack

Hadley's body went limp and I caught her, lifting her gently and settling her on the bed. God damn, the woman was fuckin' cute when she was drunk. I'd been a little concerned when she kept goin' on about how fuckin' handsome Sully was, but the second she said she thought he should have a lady friend, I knew I had nothing to be worried about.

I undressed her, leaving her in just her panties and pulling her against me as I kissed her forehead and tugged the covers over us. I loved everything about this scenario, and planned to make sure it happened again, because she obviously had a good time, and I knew she needed it.

When she woke me at four in the morning with her mouth wrapped around my cock, I decided this would happen again sooner than later.

CHAPTER
FOURTEEN

Jack

TWO WEEKS LATER, we were on our way to
Flagstaff, and then we'd move on to a few smaller
venues until we hit our biggest gig at Red Rocks
for Cramfest 2017, where we'd be sharing the bill,
not only Roses for Anna, but The Clergy, Atom Smashers,
and several other bands from back in the day. We were at
the tail end of the tour and I noticed Hadley starting to
withdraw. I didn't like it and planned to talk to her about it
once we were at the hotel.

Pulling into a roadside diner, everyone piled inside and
Lucy and Hadley sorted out seating, and that's when I noticed Ray hovering around...again. He pulled Hadley to a

table and held a chair for her. I knew she wouldn't feel comfortable saying no to him.

I was so fuckin' over him and his need to harass my woman, I started toward him, rage building.

But I was stopped.

By a petite redhead who stepped in my path.

"Uncle Jack, can I talk to you for a minute?" Lucy was suddenly standing directly in front of me.

"Uh, sure. I'm just going to go clean up really quickly."

"No, you're not," she countered.

"What?" I asked.

"Let's take a walk," she said, and quickly ushered me out the front door.

"What's going on? Why are we in the parking lot, Lucy?"

"Because, I figured you wouldn't want anyone to hear what I'm about to say, and I'm positive whatever it was you were planning on doing after marching up to your girlfriend's table wasn't going to end well for anyone."

"Girlfriend? Wait a minute, I'm not sure what you think—"

"I don't think anything. I *know* something is going on between you and Hadley. I just don't know how much has happened yet. I've been watching you two for days now, and I'm not an idiot. Before you say anything more, just know that I haven't said anything to Hadley. I didn't want to ask her and have her lie to me. Even though she's the most honest person I've ever met, I know she'd lie, because if she is with you, she'd be loyal to you. I didn't want her to have to lie for you, so I'm asking you directly. Are you and Hadley sleeping together?"

"Lucy."

"Yes or no, Jack?"

"Yes."

Lucy pursed her lips and turned around sharply in place.

She took a few deep breaths and after a few moments, slowly turned around to face me again.

"Lucy, I know this is not an ideal situation, but I promise you this isn't just a hookup for me—"

"Not ideal? More like, what the hell are the two of you thinking? Not to mention, it's one of my closest friends and my uncle. Ew!"

"Thanks a lot."

"You know what I mean, and don't change the subject," she snapped. "I've worked too hard to put this tour together and so has Hadley. And quite frankly, I'm disappointed that the both of you would put it at risk with your...your...tom foolery."

"Luce—"

"I'm not done."

It was adorable being dressed down by Lucy who I still imagined as a ten-year-old in pigtails, but I couldn't help but respect her, and as much as I didn't want to admit it, I knew she was right.

"I will agree with you that this isn't a hookup, because this thing between the two of you, whatever it is, is over."

"Wait a minute—"

She jabbed a finger toward me. "Over, Jack! She's the manager of your support act and one of my husband's most trusted friends. What exactly do you think is going to happen when they all find out?"

"Don't say anything to anyone. I'll talk to Hadley and we'll figure this out."

"I mean it, Jack, end this now or I will, for all our sakes."

"I understand."

She headed for the entrance and added, "And stay away from Ray! He's a great drum tech and I'm sure you don't want Hadley to have to hire a replacement."

I wasn't worried about his replacement; I was only worried about where I was going to hide his corpse.

* * *

Hadley

I watched distractedly out the window while Lucy gave Jack a talking to, and the reason I was distracted was because Ray would not stop talking. I'd politely laughed at his lame jokes and successfully fought back the urge to kick him under the table when he put his hand on mine.

"So, then—"

"Will you excuse me for a second?" I asked, not waiting for a reply as I slid out of the booth and walked toward Lucy.

She grabbed my hand and dragged me back outside and around the corner of the building.

"What's up?" I asked.

"Okay, I don't want to sound judgey—"

"Ohmigod, what?"

"You and Jack have to stop whatever it is you're doing."

Well, crap. "We are."

"That's not what he just led me to believe."

"Okay, wait. Lucy, I love you, you know I do, but this isn't really any of your business."

"It is if your actions drive him back into the hole that he, not to mention my family, has dug him out of."

"Wow. It's nice to know you think so little of me."

"Oh, Hadley, I'm sorry. I didn't mean it like that."

I blinked back tears. "If you think that I would do anything to jeopardize his sobriety...or anyone's for that matter, then you don't know me at all."

"I'm sorry. I'm just worried about him. He was lost after Pam, and if he gets hurt—"

"You're right. I shouldn't have been so careless." I took a big breath. "I'll see you back in there." I walked toward the front door, but headed back to the bus instead. I had a key, so I let myself in and then closed myself into the tiny bathroom, where I proceeded to sit on the lid and sob until I thought I might throw up again.

I jumped when someone banged on the door and silently screamed to myself. Could a woman not get a little privacy to deal with her broken heart?

"I'll be right out," I called as cheerily as I could.

I sat there for another few minutes, hoping the person knocking would give up and go away.

"Goddammit, Hadley, open the door," Jack snapped.

"No."

"I'll break it down if you don't."

"Don't be so melodramatic," I ground out. "I want some privacy, please."

"I'm not leavin' until you come out of there, Hadley," he warned.

"Bossy, growly, pain in the ass," I grumbled, pulling open the door.

"Why the fuck are you crying?" he snapped. "What did Lucy say?"

"Absolutely nothing she didn't say to you."

"Fuck me, it's none of her business. I have a mind to take that girl over my knee."

"Well, that would be highly inappropriate and bordering on sexual harassment." I pushed past him and headed for the door.

He grabbed my arm and turned me to face him. "Stop. We're gonna talk this out."

"There's nothing to talk about."

"Bullshit."

"Bottom line...we can't keep doing this. It needs to be over now. I've had a wonderful time with you and I hope that you have as well. I can't wait to see you play tomorrow night."

"Are you fucking kidding me?" he growled.

"What? I *am* looking forward to seeing you play." I slapped away the tears that wouldn't stop falling down my face.

"Fuck!" he snapped and dragged me away from the windows and back to the bunk room. "Come here," he said gently and pulled me against his chest.

I tried to pull away, but he held firm. "You can't do this, Jack."

"Baby, you're upset, I'm not leavin' you feelin' like shit... especially when there's no reason for it."

"I do not want to be the reason you start drinking again."

"Holy fucking Christ, is that what Lucy said?" he bellowed.

"Hadley?" Bam called.

"Damn it!" Jack snapped.

I put distance between us and tried to push him out the door. "Just go, Jack. This is over. It's better that it ends now."

"What the hell is going on?" Bam demanded.

"Nothing," I said. "It's all good. I'm PMSing and had a little bit of an emotional moment. But it's over now. You boys can go back to the restaurant. I'll be right there."

Jack scowled. "Had—"

"Jack. Go."

He let out several choice curse words then stormed off the bus. Bam did not, however.

"You gonna talk to me?" he asked, crossing his arms.

"About my PMS? That's kind of personal and not really something you need details about, is it?"

"Hadley, spill."

"Fine! Every twenty-eight days or so, the mature, unfertilized egg leaves the ovary and makes its way to the uterus via the fallopian—"

"Hadley," he snapped.

"I don't want to have this conversation with you."

"I get that, but it doesn't mean it's not gonna happen."

I bit my lip, but stayed silent.

Bam sighed. "Lucy told me what she said."

I blinked back tears. "She didn't mean it."

"That's really gracious, Hadley...not sure it's what I'd be thinkin' right now."

"Since Lucy's your wife, and you know her better than anyone, you obviously know she doesn't have a mean bone in her body, so I'm pretty sure you *would* be thinking that right now."

"Back to the subject at hand," he directed.

"No. I'm good. Just go ahead and go back inside, I'll be there in a minute."

Bam pulled me into a bear hug and even though I squirmed, he held tight. "We're gonna talk this out, Hadley. Whether you like it or not."

"We don't have time. Everyone's going to be back here in—"

"They won't be coming back on this bus until you and I have solved this crisis, so you might want to talk fast."

So, I did. I blurted everything out. Because I was sad and Bam always made everything better.

He stroked my back. "So, this is why Lucy's been antsy for the past couple of days."

"Probably," I said, dropping my face against his shoulder. "I really screwed things up, Bam."

"How so?"

"Oh, I don't know," I deadpanned. "Falling for the drummer of the headliner on a tour that could make or break Roses for Anna."

"Jesus, did you bomb Pearl Harbor as well?"

"I'm serious."

"Jack's probably got as much culpability in this as well,

Hadley, don't take this all on yourself."

"God, that makes it sound so sordid."

"Sorry, buddy," he said, giving me a gentle squeeze. "I didn't mean it like that."

I burst into tears and buried my face in his chest. "I fell in love with him, Bam, and screwed everything up. I'm so stupid."

"You're not stupid."

"I should have waited to do that 'til the end of the tour, then I could just disappear," I cried. "Now I have almost two weeks of seeing him every day and wishing..." I shook my head. "I think I'll keep that part private."

"'Preciate it, bud."

I smiled slightly and let him hold me for a few minutes. "I'm good, Bam."

"I'm not," he said.

I giggled and wrapped my arms around his waist. "You need a sisterly hug?"

"Yeah, that'd be good."

Before we could pull away, the doors to the bus opened again. "Now, what?" I whispered.

"Bam, you need to see to your wife," Jack said.

I leaned around Bam and tried to ignore the irritation on Jack's face.

"You comin'?" Bam asked.

"No. She and I are gonna talk," Jack said.

Bam craned his neck and said, "Hadley's gonna do whatever the fuck she wants to do, and you're gonna respect that."

Jack fisted his hands at his side and took several deep breaths. "Hadley, can we please talk?"

Bam looked back at me and I nodded. "Five minutes."

Bam kissed my temple, then walked off the bus, but I knew he wouldn't go far.

"Sandwich." Jack handed me a paper bag. "You puked

up your breakfast so I figured you'd be hungry."

God, he was so sweet. I had been sick that morning, but I didn't think he'd noticed. I forced back tears again, cursing my girly emotions. "Thanks, Jack."

"I talked to Lucy."

"Why?" I asked, avoiding eye-contact.

"Because what she said was both wrong and unacceptable."

"She didn't mean it, Jack. You know her."

"I don't care. My sobriety is my fuckin' business and it's my responsibility. You don't have any power in whether or not I choose to fall off the wagon. It was unfair of her to put that on you."

"I still think it's unwise of us to continue this. I think we've dodged a bullet and it would be a good idea to separate before it hurts."

"You don't think this hurts?"

"I think it hurts a lot less than if we were in love."

"Fine," he snapped. "You're probably right. I'll see you around."

He walked off the bus and I slipped back into the bathroom and sobbed for another few minutes, before I gave myself an internal talking to, stuffed my feelings then proceeded to eat them in the form of the sandwich the most wonderful man on the planet bought for me.

I died a little inside, but refused to dwell on that as the rest of the band filed onto the bus.

* * *

Jack

For the next twelve days, I proceeded to rage inside as Hadley took on the persona of Mary Fuckin' Sunshine. She had a smile for everyone but me, and I had a curt response to every question anyone asked. For the most part, folks kept their distance, but I know Rex and Roxie were watching me closely. I couldn't care less. I threw myself into my work and played better than I had before, making it easier for people to leave me alone, since no one could fault my drumming.

We had just arrived in Colorado, having already hit Southern California, Vegas, and Arizona, and we had another rare day off. This is when I got a good look at Hadley and nearly lost my mind. Fuck, she'd lost weight and I could tell she wasn't sleeping. A burning pain hit my chest like a hot poker and I realized what I'd been tryin' to shove to the side.

I was in love with her.

Completely. And because I was in love with her, the pain she was obviously experiencing cut me to the core.

I tried to get her alone, but every time I walked toward her, she'd find a reason to walk the opposite way, and by the time everyone had planned to meet at the pool, I was about to drag her back to my room and force her to eat, then sleep, then fuckin' marry me.

Since all of that was frowned upon in this century, I went looking for the only person who could help. The only other one probably watching her as closely as me.

"Bam!" I called, seeing him and Lucy heading for the side doors.

He faced me and threw a towel over his shoulder. "Hey, Jack."

"Got a minute?"

He nodded, kissed Lucy quickly, and then closed the distance between us. "What's up?"

"Is Hadley okay?"

"Not really, but that's to be expected."

"She's losing weight. I think she's sick."

He sighed. "Yeah, man, I noticed. Lucy and I forced her to go to the urgent care a few blocks from here. She actually took one of the cars about twenty minutes ago."

We had two cars with us in case we needed to go somewhere fast and didn't want to have to haul a bus some place.

"You let her go alone?" I snapped.

"Dude, there was no lettin' her do anything. She said she wouldn't go if we went with her, and since Sully's on vacation, I had Ray follow her."

I took a few deep breaths to control the rage that flooded me.

"She got there safely, Jack. It's all good. She'll tell me what's wrong when she gets back."

"Will you let me know how she is?"

"Only if she wants me to."

"Listen here, you—"

He raised a hand with a grin. "Jack, I'm sorry. I know how you feel about each other, but she's my best friend. I'm not gonna betray her trust. But I *will* let you know when she gets back here safely, okay?"

I dragged my hands down my face. I couldn't expect more from him than that, so I nodded, and then headed back to my room. Fuck me, I wanted a drink.

* * *

Hadley

The doctor was convinced everything that ailed me was altitude sickness, so I was given some oxygen and told to stop at the cantina before I headed out to eat. He took a few other tests as well, but said he'd call me with those results as soon as he had them.

The oxygen actually made me feel a lot better than I had since entering Colorado yesterday, so I was glad the doctor had been able to solve the issue so quickly. Ultimately, the only way to fully recover from altitude sickness, was to get to lower ground, but I didn't have that luxury, so the oxygen would have to solve it until we left the day after tomorrow.

I decided to forgo the cantina, dying for a bath and a nap, so I climbed in the car and pulled up my GPS, heading back to the hotel. We had less than two weeks left on the tour and I just had to get through it without another breakdown, so I could go home and lick my wounds.

Seeing Jack everywhere was killing me, but I was determined to make sure no one knew that. I cried myself to sleep every night, but during the day, I was happy.

I had to be.

For two more weeks.

Jack

FOUR HOURS LATER, there was still no sign of Hadley and I was losing my fucking mind. I couldn't sit in my room any longer, so I headed for Bam's. Pounding on the door, he opened it quickly and I pushed inside. "Where is she?"

"I don't know, man. I've been trying to reach her for an hour."

"Goddammit! Where was this clinic? I'm going there now."

"I'll go with you."

"No," I countered. "You'll stay here and call me if she shows up."

I couldn't have anyone around me right now. I was not in a good place.

Bam gave me the information, Lucy gave me keys to the SUV, and I rushed downstairs to the parking lot and took off toward the clinic.

As I pulled in, I scanned for the car Hadley had taken, but there was no sign of her, so I headed inside and pushed my way to front. "Sir, you'll need to wait your turn."

"I'm looking for Hadley Simon."

"Are you family?"

"Her husband," I lied. "She was supposed to meet me and she hasn't shown up."

"She left here almost three hours ago. I think she was going to stop in at the cantina and after that, I don't know. I actually have her test results if you'd like to take them to her."

"Yeah, I can do that." I took the paperwork from the receptionist and headed for the cantina. Hadley wasn't there, so I climbed back in the car, just as my phone buzzed. "Jack."

"Hey, man it's Bam."

"Is she there?"

"No. She's had an accident."

"What the fuck?" I slammed my hand against the steering wheel. "Where is she?"

"I'll text you the address."

I hung up and beat the shit out of the steering wheel again. "Fuck! Fuck! Fuck!"

Once Bam sent me the info, I plugged it into the GPS and pealed out of the parking lot, daring any cop who might make the mistake of pulling me over for speeding.

* * *

Hadley

"Ma'am?"

I forced my heavy lids open, frustrated because it hurt to open my eyes...my head was pounding so hard.

"There you are," a kind voice said. "Can you squeeze my fingers?"

I did as she asked, losing my fight with wakefulness again.

"Ma'am, stay with me."

"I can't..."

"We're gonna give you something for the pain, but I need you to open your eyes."

"Where...?" I forced my eyes open again.

"You're at the hospital. You've had an accident."

"What?" I rasped.

Something was shoved in my nose and I grimaced.

"It's just oxygen, honey. Breathe deeply."

A bright light hit my pupils and I cried out.

"Pupils responsive," a male voice said.

"What's your name, honey?"

"Hadley Simon," I said, swallowing.

"Do you know what day it is?"

"Thursday." I frowned. "Why am I in the hospital?"

"You ran your car into a lamppost."

"What?" I squeaked. "Was anyone hurt?"

"Just you, honey. It's okay, we're just checking you out now."

I tried to find the voice, but I couldn't get my eyes to cooperate.

"Have you had anything to drink?" a male voice asked.

"No. I was feeling sick, so I went to the urgent care. They said I had altitude sickness," I said.

I groaned when something pricked my arm, then a soft

hand rubbed my hand. "Just an IV, sweetie. We're gonna get some fluids into you."

"Is there someone we can call?"

"Yes," I whispered. "Beau Nelson." I rattled off the phone number and then my pain suddenly subsided and I sank further into the plastic mattress.

About an hour later, my eyelids finally felt less like sandpaper, but my head still pounded.

"Knock, knock." An older doctor walked in and made his way to my bed.

"Hi, doctor," I said.

"How's our patient, then?"

"My head is killing me."

"The IV should take care of your dehydration, which will help, and those pain meds should do the rest once they've kicked in. I've run a series of complete diagnostics so we can best determine why you passed out. Just sit tight and we'll take good care of you while we wait for the results. You just try to get some rest and I'll be back in just a bit."

* * *

Jack

I parked (probably illegally) and rushed into the emergency room and to the nurses' desk. "Hadley Simon. Is she here?"

"I'll have a look, sir. Just give me a second."

This all took a hell of a lot longer than I wanted to wait. "Damn it, lady, where the hell is she?"

"Sir, I need you to calm down."

I took a few deep breaths, knowing that if I threatened the woman, I'd never be able to see Hadley.

"Are you family?"

"Husband," I lied again.

"Okay, sir. I'll see what I can find out."

"Is she here or isn't she?" I snapped.

"She is, but I need to get the doctor to come and speak to you."

"Is she okay?"

"I don't know her status. I'm sorry," she said.

"Goddammit," I rasped, dragging my hands down my face. My heart raced and my stomach roiled. I couldn't deal with her being hurt or...worse.

"Sir?"

I spun to face an older man in a white coat and tried not to take him by the collar and demand answers.

"Are you Hadley Sim—"

"Yes. How is she?"

"She had a pretty nasty accident, but all-in-all, she's doing well. Concussion and a few bruises, but nothing's broken. We're going to keep her in here overnight for observation."

"Can I see her?"

"Yes. I'll show you to her room."

I followed the doctor down the hall and he pushed open the door and ushered me inside. Hadley was sleeping, but she looked so small in the large bed, and her face was marred with several bruises.

"The airbags did their job, but she did get a few bruises from the blast and the seatbelt."

I tried not to lose my shit staring at her motionless body on the mattress. She had an oxygen mask on and she just looked wrecked.

"She'll be sleeping for a little bit, but you can stay with her. We've run a few tests, so once those results are in, I'll come back and fill everyone in."

Shit! I left her paperwork in the truck.

"Thanks, Doc," I said, and he left me alone with her. I dragged a chair to her bedside and took her hand in mine, lifting it my lips and kissing her palm. "I'm here, baby."

* * *

Hadley

My head felt like someone was slamming an icepick into it. I heard myself groan and then a rough hand squeezed mine. "I got you, baby," Jack said. "Open your pretty eyes for me, will you?"

"It hurts."

"I know, honey. Try."

He squeezed my hand again and I forced my gritty eyelids open. Jack hovered over me, looking like he'd aged a decade since this morning.

He smiled. "Hey, baby."

"What are you doing here?" I shifted with a grimace and he sat on the edge of the bed.

"Well, you weren't at the clinic, so I had to find you."

"I apparently passed out and crashed the car." I blinked back tears. "I'm so sorry, Jack. I'll pay for the damage."

"You're not gonna worry about the fuckin' car, Hadley, you're gonna worry about you."

"Why are you here?"

"Because I love you."

"What?" I squeaked.

"I've been an ass," he said. "I should have told you sooner, but I've been tryin' to fight it. I love you, Hadley, with every fiber of my being. I can't live without you and I want to figure out how to make this work."

I burst into tears which totally fucked with my head, but I couldn't help it. I was so happy...and sad...and confused.

"Baby, do you love me? Or am I sittin' here makin' a fool of myself."

"No. I love you. I love you so much it hurts."

He leaned down and kissed me gently and I gingerly wrapped my arms around him and held him as tightly as my

IV would allow.

Jack stroked my cheek and kissed me again. "Did you find out what was wrong at the clinic?"

"Sort of."

"What did they say?"

"Altitude sickness is definitely part of it."

"We should probably get you out of Colorado, then."

I nodded.

He kissed my palm. "You gonna marry me?"

"You haven't asked."

"You want me to do something romantic?"

I burst into tears and Jack's face dropped. "Baby, what?"

I shook my head. I had no words. I just couldn't process anything in my drug-induced state.

"You're scarin' me, Hadley. You need to fill me in here, babe."

"I'm..."

"You're...?"

I took a deep breath and squeezed his hand.

"Baby, tell me. Are you okay? You can tell me anything," he urged.

"I'm fine Jack...and so is the baby."

"The baby? You mean...you're..."

"I'm pregnant."

"Holy shit," Jack breathed out.

"We were so careful," I whispered.

"Apparently, not careful enough."

"I'm so sorry."

"Why the fuck are you sorry?"

I squeezed my eyes shut. "Because you didn't sign up for that."

"Baby, look at me."

I forced myself to meet his eyes and the love I saw in

155

them humbled me to my core.

"I love you. I'm all in. I want you to have my babies, I want you to raise kids with you. I want it all," he said. "This is something I could never allow myself to dream for, don't you understand that? You're giving me more than I deserve. I couldn't love you more."

"Jack."

He kissed my palm. "Promise me you'll marry me, and I'll surprise you with a ring to die for."

I smiled through watery eyes. "Okay, Jack. I'll marry you, *if* you give me a ring to die for."

"Good, because I kind of told them you were my wife so I could get in here."

"You *didn't*."

"I did." He leaned over me again. "I love you, baby."

I pulled him down to kiss me. "I love you so much, Jack Henry. God, you're just too much, even if my last name is now going to be Gornitzka."

He laughed, kissing me again and again. "We could legally change both our names to something completely different."

"No, I love all of you, so I'm happy to be a Gornitzka."

"Hadley Gornitzka…"

"It's better than Hadley Henry."

He grinned. "I kinda like that, Hadley."

I kind of did, too, but his name was his name and I wanted to honor that. I smiled and stroked his cheek. "I kinda like *you*."

"Kinda like you too, baby." He stroked my cheek, then took my hand in his again. "Where do you want to live?"

"Wow, straight to it, huh?"

"Not wastin' anymore time. Been there, done that."

Before I could respond, a nurse walked in wheeling a medical device. She smiled and made her way to the bed.

"We're going to give you an ultrasound to check the baby. Is that okay?"

"Holy shit," Jack rasped.

I nodded. "That's great."

"Is this the father?" the nurse asked.

"Yes." I squeezed his hand. "The very surprised daddy."

"Well, I hope it's a good surprise."

"Very good," Jack said.

"Great. Doc'll be in shortly and we can check out that baby."

"Thank you," I said, and the nurse walked out, but returned quickly with another doctor.

They prepped everything, and once Jack calmed down after seeing the wand they planned to stick inside of me, the doctor took some images, declared baby was doing well, the heartbeat was strong, and we'd be holding our little boy or girl in about eight months.

This meant, I'd pretty much gotten pregnant right away. I was a little overwhelmed with this thought, but tried to remember Jack was here with me…not running for the hills.

"You okay?" Jack asked, pulling my focus back to him.

"I'm good, honey. Just tired."

He leaned over me and kissed me gently. "Sleep. I'm not going anywhere." He moved to my belly and kissed it. "Hey, baby. It's daddy. Can't wait to meet you."

My tears started again, but this time I wasn't scared as Jack kissed me again and I succumbed to sleep.

* * *

The next morning, I awoke to a room full of people. I instinctively reached for Jack who grabbed my hand gently and squeezed.

"Hey, baby," he said.

Lucy rushed to me and gave me a hug. "Ohmigod, Had, I'm so sorry!"

"About what?"

"Everything," she whispered.

"It's okay, honey."

Roxie hugged me next, but Rex just gave me a nod and a smile from across the room. "I'm really sorry about the car, Rex."

"Don't even worry about it," he said. "Always hated that thing."

Bam leaned down and kissed my cheek. "You look like shit."

"Thanks, buddy."

"Anytime." He smiled. "Really glad you're okay."

I smiled up at him. "Me too, honey."

Jack squeezed my hand again, then linked his fingers with mine.

"What are y'all doing here?" I asked. "Aren't you supposed to be over at the Amphitheatre?"

"You're a little more important than load-in," Rex said.

Well, that made me feel all gooey and sweet. "Thank you. But I'm good." I looked up at Jack. "They're releasing me soon, so you guys should go."

"I'm not goin' anywhere, Hadley."

"Jack—"

He squeezed my hand. "Not up for discussion."

"Someone gonna fill me in on this?" Rex asked.

"I'm going to stay with Hadley until she's released, then I'm checking her into a hotel, where I can take care of her."

"Does that mean the world's worst kept secret is finally out?" Rex asked.

"Don't tease her, Rex." Roxie smacked his stomach lightly. "Ignore him, Hadley."

"If you all knew, why didn't you say something?" I asked Roxie.

"Rex told me he and Jack talked…"

My head snapped towards Jack.

"I told him there was nothing between us!" Jack rushed to say.

"Which was a lie and I knew it." Rex smiled.

"Alright, 'Junior Detective Squad,' here's something you don't know," Jack said. "Hadley and I are getting married."

"Jack," I whispered, squeezing my eyes shut. I just wanted to crawl into a hole and hide.

I don't know why I'd been so worried. The room erupted in hoots and hollers, and I was suddenly being hugged by everyone including Rex.

Jack looked down at me and raised an eyebrow. I nodded and he smiled wide.

"And here's another newsflash...we're havin' a baby." Jack beamed and the room once again was filled with cheers and hugs, albeit a little gentler this time.

Once they were done with me, they turned to Jack, and I watched in awe as his family surrounded him with genuine excitement. Jack shushed everyone, declaring I needed quiet, then sat beside me again and took my hand.

"We really need to get to the venue," Lucy said.

"I'm not leaving Hadley."

"Honey, you have a show," I argued. "You have to play."

"I don't have to do shit," he ground out. "Bam can fill it."

"What's this now?" Bam breathed out.

"You know all our songs, and you watch our show from the side of the stage every night?" Jack said.

"Yeah, but—"

"Well, who better for the job?" Jack asked.

"Do you mind doing it?" Roxie asked.

Bam crossed his arms. "No, of course not but, it's Cramfest, and I'm not Jack Henry.

"He's not so special," I retorted, and Jack laughed.

"You *do* know all the songs, honey," Lucy said.

"We'll meet you in Idaho," Jack said. "Hadley needs to get out of this altitude and I need a break from all this hugging."

I was surprised how little convincing it took to get everyone to accept the fact Jack wouldn't be at the biggest show of their tour. In the end, I think we all just knew Jack and when he made up his mind, there was no changing it.

The next morning, I was released and Jack loaded me into a rental car and we took off to lower ground.

CHAPTER SIXTEEN

Jack

BY THE TIME we reached the hotel in Boise, it was almost two o'clock in the morning. I'd driven straight through Wyoming and Idaho, with Hadley sleeping by my side, stopping only when absolutely necessary. She clearly needed the rest, and I had never been more at peace. The vastness of the Wyoming sky stretching endlessly over the plains was breathtaking. Its beauty was only rivaled by the woman sleeping in the seat next to me.

"Where are we?" Hadley asked, with a stretch and a yawn.

"We're here."

"Here where?" she asked. "The hotel?"

"Nope, Disneyland. I figure we have just enough time for a couple of spins on Space Mountain. Yeah, the hotel." She looked around, then back at me. "Wow, I can't believe how much I slept. I usually can't sleep at all in cars."

"You're getting used to road life," I lifted her palm to my lips. "How are you feeling?"

"Much better. I'm actually surprised by what a difference the lower altitude makes."

"Come on, Sleeping Beauty, I'll help you out of the car."

I walked Hadley to the lobby, sat her down and returned to the car to get our bags. When I returned, she was staring intensely at her phone.

"You'd better not be working," I said as I rolled our bags through the lobby.

"My phone was off."

"Yeah, it was buzzing every thirty seconds, and I didn't want it to wake you, so I turned it off."

"Apparently Buzzfeed and TMZ got wind of you being MIA for Cramfest and the promoter is freaking out."

"Jimbo can freak out all he wants, I don't give a shit," I said.

"No, you don't understand. He's saying the package was sold as an 'all original members' reunion, and that by having Bam fill in, you're failing to meet the contract's obligations."

"So, he's threatening not to pay us for the Red Rocks show?" I set the bags next to Hadley.

She scanned her phone. "Not only that, but he's threatening to cancel the remaining two shows of the tour if you don't show up tonight."

"He's bluffing."

"Maybe so" —she looked up at me with a sigh— "but Lucy's having to deal with all this on her own, because

Bam is off learning every one of your drum fills, note-for-note."

I chuckled. "I don't even know all my drum fills note-for-note. Maybe I'll have him show me when we get back."

"Would you please be serious?" Hadley smacked my arm.

"I am serious. Serious about you getting some serious rest. Seriously. Now give me your phone."

"I don't need rest. I just slept for a bajillion hours, and the tour is in trouble." She met my eyes. "This is my job, Jack."

"I understand, but you have another job right now that's more important. Your job is to let me keep you and our baby safe and healthy, so how about we get checked in, go up to our room, and I'll draw you a nice warm bath? We'll figure out what to do about the tour after that."

Hadley relented and we settled into our room. As promised, I drew her a bath, and flopped down on the bed while she soaked. I needed to rest my eyes for just a few minutes.

I awoke five hours later...alone.

* * *

Hadley

The minute I heard Jack snoring, I bolted out of the tub, got dressed, grabbed my phone and day planner, and headed for the lobby. There was no way I could sleep when I knew Lucy was awake and probably stressing. I wasn't about to leave her, or the bands, high and dry. I called her right away and she answered on the first ring.

"Hi, Had," she whispered. "Give me a sec."

I heard a door close and then Lucy said, "Hey, I'm here."

"How's Bam?" I asked.

"Stressed."

"What's to be stressed about?" I retorted. "He's only stepping into his hero's shoes, at one of the biggest rock festivals of the year, on twenty-four hours' notice."

"Without his manager and best bud by his side," Lucy added with a quiet giggle.

"He's got you, I'm sure he's fine."

"He doesn't want to let anybody down, least of all Jack."

I sighed. "Jack wouldn't have asked him if he didn't have his full confidence."

"I wish everyone else shared in his sentiment."

I frowned. "What? Who doesn't?"

"When the news that Jack wasn't playing the show, and that Bam would be filling in, hit the internet, the usual war between the fans and the trolls started on all the message boards."

"He can't pay attention to that garbage."

"That's what I told him, but the naysayers had gotten under his skin already and now there's the added stress of Jimbo's tirade."

"How's that all going?" I asked.

"A little better. I was able to roll him back to DEFCON 4 with the help of a really nice bottle of scotch and a reminder of the money he'd lose by pulling the plug on the tour. It took a while, but by the time we were done, I had Uncle Jimbo right where I wanted him."

"You are such a badass, Lucy."

"Well, this badass has been up all night and has a big day ahead of her, so I'm gonna get a little rest. You should do the same."

"I'm wired now," I admitted. "So I think I'm going to find some breakfast. Call me later and let me know how everything's going."

"I will."

I smiled. "Thanks for everything, honey. I really appreciate it."

"You can owe me one," Lucy said.

"Done."

She hung up and I headed to the restaurant attached to the hotel. After being seated, I ordered coffee and breakfast and then set out to go through my notes and see if there was a way to support Lucy more than I was right now.

The minute my coffee arrived, a rough hand settled on the back of my neck and an angry voice whispered in my ear, "I really hope this image of my woman eating breakfast alone is a figment of my imagination. Because *my* woman, who is pregnant and sick, wouldn't leave me in our bed and not tell me where she was going."

I rolled my eyes. "I didn't want to wake you."

"Hadley," he growled.

"Look, baby, I'm eating," I said, trying to distract his irritation.

He sat across from me. "I don't see food, Had—"

Before he'd gotten my name past his lips, the server arrived and slid a plate stacked with eggs, bacon, hash browns, and pancakes in front of me.

I gave him a triumphant grin. "Want some?"

"Coffee," he said to the waitress who nodded and walked away. He faced me and leaned forward. "Don't do that again."

I wrinkled my nose as I shoved a bite of pancakes in my mouth and chewed.

He sat there for a few seconds before he sighed and his expression of irritation was replaced with a smile. "Fuck me, you're gorgeous."

"Thank you." I swallowed and gave him a cheeky grin. "Seriously, do you want some?"

"You can't eat all of that?"

"I'm gonna give it the good ol' college try."

"I'll order something else," he said, and grabbed the

menu.

I leaned over the table and grabbed his hand. "I'm sorry I worried you, honey."

"Appreciate that, baby. Next time leave a note."

I smiled. "I will."

He slid out of his seat and sat beside me, pulling me close and kissing me. "Hey."

I grinned. "Hi, honey."

He licked his lips, he said, "Syrupy and sweet," then kissed me again.

"We might need to borrow some of that...for later."

He growled low, kissing me again. "If you didn't need to eat, I'd take you back to the room and fuck you senseless."

I slid one of my hands up his thigh and stopped close to his cock. "There's no reason why we couldn't eat, steal some syrup, then take it upstairs." I smiled, sliding my hand a little higher. "But you have to promise to lick this off of me."

He dropped his head back and groaned. "Fuck me, Hadley, you really doin' this to me right now?"

"You were rude, so yes."

"Hold up." He met my eyes again. "You're sayin' because I came down pissed that you left me in bed and worried the hell out of me, you're going to reciprocate with dirty sex and letting me lick syrup off your pussy?"

"I didn't say pussy," I whispered. "But that's even better, so yes."

He grunted out a laugh and cupped my cheek. "This is working for me."

"Me too," I admitted.

"We'll eat quick."

I nodded, sliding my finger through the syrup on my plate, then licking it.

"Baby, stop," he demanded.

"Only if you promise I get to do that to your—"

"Hadley," he snapped, and moved to the other seat again.

I giggled. "Killjoy."

"I haven't even seen the depths of your evilness, have I?"

"Not even close," I retorted as I took another bite of pancakes.

He chuckled and his food arrived a few seconds later, so we ate as quickly as we could and then headed upstairs to use the sugary sweetness we'd pilfered from the restaurant.

Our plans were blown to hell, however, when morning sickness reared its ugly head and I couldn't keep anything down. Jack grabbed a brush and pulled my hair back into a scrunchy, lovingly stroking my back as I lay in the fetal position in bed.

"I felt so good this morning," I complained.

"I'm sorry, baby. As soon as you feel a little better, I'll run to the store and grab you saltines and ginger ale."

"Can you find a pharmacy and see what they suggest for morning sickness?"

"Of course."

I sighed. "I love you."

He shifted and stretched out behind me, kissing the nape of my neck. "I don't like that you're sick."

I chuckled. "You're gonna be hatin' life for a while, then."

"Yep." He rubbed my back again. "I can't believe we're havin' a baby."

I rolled to face him. "Are you sure you're okay with all of this?"

"I'm better than okay."

"Really?"

"Why the worry?" he asked.

"I just figure, you've been with no one serious since

Pam, and since I don't know whether or not you chose not to have kids or it just happened that way...I don't know, I'm a girl. We spiral."

He stroked my cheek. "So, let's get this out of the way, then, yeah?"

I nodded.

"Pam and I never had kids, mostly because we always thought there'd be time. Back then, our life was a constant party, and we didn't want anything to fuck with it. But I also think there was a part of her that was concerned about me and my addictions. She didn't say anything, because she could be a little passive at times, but when I reflect on that part of our relationship, it's what I surmise. I loved her, Hadley, but don't get me wrong, we had our issues."

"Doesn't everyone?"

"Sure. But we wouldn't have survived rehab."

"You don't think so?"

He shook his head. "We masked our issues with drugs and alcohol, and then when she got sick, I sobered up for a little while...a very little while. I couldn't deal. With anything, so I raged. It was easier than to face what was coming. I pushed everyone away, except her. But she knew. She tried to talk to me, but I was able to change the subject...or she let me...either way, we weren't always on the same page. I'm surprised Rex and Roxie didn't kick me to the curb...well, Roxie mostly because Rex and I both went into rehab right after Pam died."

"Roxie seems like a saint."

"Yeah...except the sailor's mouth."

I giggled. "That just makes her more interesting."

"This is true."

"Did Pam want kids?"

"Yeah, but not as much as I did."

"Really?"

He nodded. "Pam liked our life. I did, too, but I always

wanted to add to it. She was hesitant."

I ran my fingers down his beard. "I'm sorry, honey."

He grinned, turning his head to kiss my palm. "Don't be. You're making a dream come true, Hadley. I wasn't quite sure how I'd get this particular dream, but you know, I wouldn't change it."

"You wouldn't?"

"Nope. Because it's one I couldn't have planned for, mostly because I'd thought it was dead. You're the dream I thought was lost, Hadley."

I sighed, leaning forward to kiss him gently. "I love you, Jack Henry Gornitzka."

"Love you too, baby." He kissed my forehead. "I'm gonna go get you some supplies, okay?"

"That would be amazing. I feel a lot better, but that probably won't last."

"Promise me you won't move."

I nodded. "I'll do my best."

"Do my best, baby...not yours."

"Oh, you're funny. You should add stand-up to your shows."

He chuckled and kissed me again before leaving me in the bed.

Jack

I WALKED BACK into our room to find Hadley sacked out, her quiet snore music to my ears, knowing she needed the rest. Setting the bags on the counter, I grabbed my laptop and ear buds, and sat on the sofa to check a few emails.

I wasn't quite prepared for what I found. The word was out that Bam would be playing drums for RatHound tonight and the internet was buzzing. Apparently, Lucy was able to smooth things over with the promoters, and all was going well, but I felt a little bad for Bam. I knew he was going to do a great job, and would eventually have fun, but I also figured he was probably a nervous wreck right now.

I finished up responding to email and closed my laptop. I wanted to focus as much of my attention on Hadley as possible. I'd put work before my marriage in the past, and wasn't going to make the same mistake twice. I would have never trusted anyone else in my drum stool back in the day. I would have found some way to justify being on stage tonight, no matter what, but at this moment, I wanted to watch Hadley sleep more than I wanted to hear the roar of the crowd. I wanted to think about the future with my new family more than I wanted the road.

* * *

"Have you been watching me the whole time?" Hadley asked as she stretched.

"You're so beautiful when you sleep, I couldn't help it."

"Beautiful when I sleep?"

"Oh yes, very beautiful. Except when you drool," I teased.

"I do not drool."

"You most certainly do. It's disgusting," I said, leaning down to kiss her.

"I do not." She turned her head to avoid my kiss. "Now take that back or else."

"Or else what?" I challenged.

"Or I won't kiss you anymore."

"You wouldn't dare."

She raised an eyebrow. "Oh, I would."

"Even though you'd really be the one missing out."

"Full of yourself much?" Hadley laughed.

"I'd rather you be full of me."

"Well that's off the table too, mister, until you take it back."

"Okay, fine I take it back, you don't drool when you

sleep...just snore."

Hadley hit me with her pillow and I pounced on her, kissing her neck and tickling her.

"Stop! I'm gonna pee!" she cried out as I continued my attack.

"You're cute when you laugh, baby." I laughed and she grabbed my arms.

"Seriously, honey, I'm going to pee. Let me up."

I jumped off the bed immediately and she slid her feet off the mattress.

"Slow, baby," I said. I steadied her and frowned. "You sick?"

"Not yet."

"You want stuff for the nausea now or wait?"

"We should probably do now," she said. "Just to be safe."

I grabbed the bags of groceries, and she took an anti-nausea pill with a little ginger ale and a saltine.

After a few minutes, she pushed off the bed and headed to the bathroom. I followed, concerned she might pass out again.

"I'm okay, honey," she said.

I studied her. "You dizzy? At all?"

"Not even a little bit."

"Okay, sweetness, just be careful."

She leaned up and kissed me. "I will."

We decided to eat in the hotel's dining room for dinner and were seated by a grand fireplace, which was currently illuminated by a series of large candles, rather than flaming logs, I assumed to keep the heat down in the summer months. The dining room wasn't very busy and we were enjoying our quiet, romantic meal...well...until...

"Excuse me, Jack Henry?"

I looked up to see a woman in her late-forties, wearing thick cat's eye frames, holding a RatHound 1995 tour program and several CDs.

"Yeah…on my better days," I said, and gave the woman a smile.

Rather than looking pleased, the woman actually looked like she was in total agony. Her body shook and she began to make a low groaning sound. Eventually, her noises began to sound like words. Normally, I hated when people interrupted me for a picture or an autograph…it's part of the reason I grew my hair long. Once I did that, people recognized me less and less, but apparently, the word was out and my cover was blown. It had been a while, and I was in a good mood, so I decided not to blow her off.

"Ohmigod, ohmigod, ohmigod, I'm your b-b-biggest fan."

"Oh, yeah?"

She bobbed her head up and down and let out a strange moaning sound. "I knew Rex would come to his senses and put the band back together."

This woman was a weirdo.

"Did you want me to sign those for you?" I asked, motioning to her stack of RatHound merch.

She simply moaned again and quickly thrust the items toward me.

"Who should I make this out to?" I asked.

"Uh…Cathy…I'm Cathy…I'm Cathy Meadows."

"It's nice to meet you."

"We've met, Jack."

"Yeah?"

"It's been a long time, so you might not remember."

"Maybe not." I nodded toward Hadley. "This is my fiancé, Hadley."

Cathy stopped smiling. In fact, Cathy stopped moving altogether. Her unblinking gaze was now fully set on Hadley.

"Where are you from, Cathy?" I asked in an attempt to

turn her focus back to me, or at least back to earth.

"I'm from Colorado," she said without breaking her focus on Hadley.

"What a coincidence," I said, signing her things. "We were just in Colorado."

"I know."

I tried again. "What brings you to Boise?"

She finally turned to me and said, "You."

I looked at Hadley, and her eyes were as big as saucers. I swallowed hard and hoped Cathy didn't notice. This chick was seriously starting to freak me the fuck out.

"I'm here to see you guys play at the Idaho Center Arena," she said.

"Wow, you're in town a little...early aren't you? The show's not for another two days."

"I was going to see you at Red Rocks tonight, but when I heard you weren't going to be playing drums, I drove straight here instead."

"Last night?" Hadley asked.

"Uh huh," Cathy answered.

My blood ran cold. "How did you...know I was at this particular hotel?"

"I saw you pull in here when I was following you."

* * *

Hadley

What the hell? This woman was nuts.

If looks could kill, I'd be dead ten times over, and considering I'd seen what women could do to other women who got between them and their idols, she was making me more than a little nervous.

"What room are you in?" Cathy asked.

"We don't give that kind of information out, Cathy," Jack said.

I just sat there dumbfounded considering I couldn't believe she'd even asked.

"Is there anything I can do for you?" She stepped closer, apparently, now feeling more comfortable. "I can run errands, um, and, ah, things. Whatever you need."

"We've got it handled," Jack said.

She pulled a chair up to the table and plopped herself down between us. "I can't believe I'm having dinner with Jack Henry."

"Cathy, I'm sorry, but you can't join us."

"Oh, how come? I've come all this way and I'm all by myself."

I raised my eyebrow at Jack. I'd like to see how he got out of this one.

"Well, I'm here with my fiancée, and…"

"Oh, she doesn't bother me," Cathy said.

I choked on the sip of water I'd just taken and Jack gave me a look of panic.

"Sorry, will you excuse me for a second?" I said, and stood.

Jack shook his head, and I escaped…heading straight for the front desk.

"Miss Simon?" a voice said from behind me and I turned to see Rolf, the general manager approaching me.

"Hi, Rolf."

"Can I help you with something?"

"Um, yes, please, if you wouldn't mind. Jack's having a little problem with a fan."

I filled him in on Cathy and her desire to sit with him…but I left out the fact that she probably wanted to make a skin suit out of him.

"I'll take care of it," Rolf said. "Just head on back to dinner."

The fact that the bands had pretty much booked out the hotel for the next two nights, meant we got a little extra preferential treatment. Rolf was close to Jack's age, so I had an inkling he was a fan... probably a secret one...but, regardless, I appreciated whatever he could do to keep the crazies from my man.

"Thank you." Instead of heading straight back to the table, I made a pitstop, then joined Jack again, who was still dealing with Cathy. And she appeared to have moved closer to him.

Jack stood, reaching his hand out as though to grab me like a lifeline. "Hi, baby."

I grinned, sliding against his body. "Hi, honey."

Cathy looked like she might explode, but I didn't object when Jack sat in the chair furthest away from her and settled me between them.

Our server arrived and smiled at Cathy. "Are you Ms. Meadows?"

"Yes."

"Oh, you have a phone call."

She frowned. "Here?"

"Yes, ma'am."

Her frown turned into a scowl, but she didn't move to get up.

"It's quite urgent," the waitress stressed.

"Ah, okay, right." Cathy rose to her feet and the waitress led her away, returning quickly with a grin.

"She won't bother you again."

Jack sighed. "Thank you."

"Not a problem." She smiled. "Can I bring you anything?"

"Cheesecake," I said.

She grinned. "I can do that."

"I'll have coffee, please," Jack said.

The waitress nodded and walked away.

"Do you think she'll come back?" Jack whispered.

"Why are you whispering?"

"In case she's, I don't know, a witch or something."

I burst out laughing. "Is whispering a thing...with witches?"

He rolled his eyes. "I'm not taking any chances."

"Well, she won't be back."

"How do you know?"

I patted my chest. "Because, I'm Hadley Freakin' Simon and I took care of it."

He leaned over and kissed me...hard. "I love you. Holy fuckin' hell, she was nuts."

"I'm sorry, honey." I smiled and stroked his cheek. "My big, bad, sexy man can't handle one crazy, fifty-something lady? It's okay, your woman's here to protect you."

He chuckled, leaning forward to kiss me again. "You're cute, you know that?"

"I sure do."

He ran his thumb over my bottom lip. "Thank you for taking care of me."

"Always, honey."

He kissed me again and the waitress returned with our dessert. By the time we were ready to pay for the meal, I could barely keep my eyes open.

Jack held me close as we headed back to our room and I couldn't help but notice Cathy wasn't lurking anywhere. Well, anywhere that I could see, anyway.

Maybe she *was* a witch.

Arriving at our room, Jack closed us in to the quiet, and I undressed quickly and practically fell into bed.

"You want to take another pill?" he asked.

"No, I'm good," I said, biting back a yawn. "Just exhausted."

"Take your prenatal."

I groaned. "Okay, I'll do that."

He handed me the pill and I took it, then crawled back under the covers. I felt the bed dip when Jack climbed in beside me, but don't remember anything after that.

* * *

Ohmigod, I was dying. I was sure of it.

I sat up, disoriented for a second, then remembered where I was, and made a mad dash for the toilet. I should have forgone the prenatal...or taken it sooner. God! My stomach was on the rampage.

"Baby?" Jack whispered from the doorway.

"It's okay, I'm okay. The baby's just trying to kill me."

He gave me a sad chuckle and hunkered down beside me. "I'm sorry, baby."

"It's okay." I dropped my head to my arms on the seat. "It'll all be worth it."

"Yes, it will be." He rubbed my back for a second and then stood. "I'll get you some ginger ale."

"Thanks."

I pushed myself away from the ground, washed my hands, and sat on the edge of the bed. Jack handed me a pill and a can of soda and I smiled up at him. "Don't let me stop you from shoving a pill down my throat next time, okay?"

He smiled. "I got your back, baby. Don't worry."

"I think I got cocky."

"Yeah?"

I nodded. "I ate all of dinner and that to-die-for cheesecake and thought I was in the clear."

"We'll know better next time."

I yawned. "I'm going to brush my teeth, then I'm going to die."

Jack waited for me to return, then climbed in beside me and pulled me close.

"You sure you want to risk this?" I challenged.

"Yeah, baby. I'm good."

I kissed his chest. "Okay, honey. I love you."
"Love you too."
I closed my eyes and succumbed to sleep.

CHAPTER
EIGHTEEN

Jack

OUR MINI GETAWAY wasn't quite what I'd hoped for, but it was good to rest, and great being alone with Hadley. I'd hoped we'd be able to talk more about our future over dinner, but our uninvited guest sort of derailed that. After that, I just wanted to keep things light and restful for Hadley. I could tell she had something on her mind, and could only assume she had questions and fears about our future, but I didn't quite know how to approach things with her just yet. She was still a relative stranger to me in so many ways, which was odd because my heart knew her completely.

There had been no sign of Cathy on the road, and believe me, my head was on a swivel. Hadley spoke with venue security the moment we got here. These days, you can never be too careful, and I was of the opinion that Cathy Meadows was a few tacos short of a fiesta plate.

We walked through the backstage halls of the arena, which is about a twelve hundred seat venue that we'd apparently sold out. In fact, the entire tour had sold out, which was more satisfying than I thought it would be. Maybe it's because I didn't expect it or even think about it.

"Well, look who decided to show up! Didn't you get the notice that you've been replaced?" Rex yelled through the throngs of people in the dressing room. Backstage always seemed to get a little more crowded as tours went on, so now that we were just two dates from the end of the tour, it was a bit of a zoo tonight.

Through the masses I spotted Bam sitting on the couch with his bassist, Jimmy.

"At least my replacement is a complete bad ass!" I replied.

The dressing room erupted in applause and Bam smiled wide, and bowed his head in humility. "Thank y'all, you're too kind. Really, thank you, you can kindly all shut the fuck up now!" Bam joked.

The room was filled with laughter and the party resumed. Bam stood to his feet and we embraced.

"Seriously, Bam, thank you," I said. "You totally saved my ass, and everyone who saw the show says you killed it. I appreciate you being there for me, and most importantly, for Hadley."

"I'd do anything for her. Hadley's my family, and if you're getting married and havin' a kid with her, that makes you my family. Not to mention, that was my childhood fantasy, so I should be thanking you. I still can't believe it happened, and I'm pretty much in shock, and now I'm babbling. I need a beer." Bam met my eyes. "Oh, shit! Sorry man, I—"

"It's okay." I laughed. "I'm happy it worked out for both of us and thank you again. I owe you one."

"That means something where I'm from," he said earnestly, his southern drawl pouring out.

"It doesn't mean shit where I'm from, but it does to me, so ask it and you've got it."

We talked more about the show and how he felt about it. It was interesting to get another drummer's thoughts on playing in my band, with my bandmates. It was fun talking with Bam. He was a natural storyteller and a straight shooter. He had a very unique perspective about what it was like to hitch up to the animals that are Rex and Robbie, which I got a kick out of hearing.

"It was brutal at first," Bam laughed. "We couldn't soundcheck because of the whole festival thing. The Clergy was on right before us, and it was a pretty tight turnaround before we were on."

"I bet it felt like forever," I said.

"Exactly the opposite! Before I knew it, Ray was handing me my sticks, I sat down and we were off."

"First thought?" I asked.

"Loud...as...fuck."

I laughed.

"You must be deaf," he said.

"What?"

"Seriously," he continued. "I've never been on stage with guys playing that loud before. I thought my band cranked, but holy shit brother. Even through my in-ears, I could hear Rex and Robbie's rigs."

"Robbie still uses wedges," I said. "We're from another time man, a very loud time."

We talked a while longer and I made note of his keen

sense of people and what they were thinking. He seemed not only street smart, but wise for his age.

I made a note to pick his brain some time about Hadley, as her closest friend, he likely had a similar vantage point into her as he did with my band. It's not like I couldn't talk to her directly, I just figured I'd use any solid help I could get into understanding the woman that was going to be my wife and the mother of my child.

I mingled among the celebrities, press people, and various backstage guests for about another hour and then headed out to find my five-foot-five-inch fix.

It was a bit strange being thrust right back into band chaos after a few days of relative isolation, and as much as I sparked from being back 'in it,' while mingling, I was mostly thinking of the next time I'd be alone with Hadley again. I was so preoccupied with her, that had it not been for the roadies running past me in the halls, and the rumble crowd growing louder by the moment, I might have even forgotten I had a show to play tonight.

* * *

Hadley

I was standing in the corner…and I was in the corner because Ray was boxing me in…and all I could think about was getting the hell away from him. He'd piled on a little more cologne than normal (or I just happened to notice because every smell elicited a physical and sometimes violent response from me).

"So, this thing with Jack," Ray said. "It's serious?"

"Ah, yeah, very."

"You sure?"

"She's fuckin' sure, Ray, now walk away," Jack growled as he moved between us.

"Dude!" Ray said, raising his hands. "Just askin'."

"And now you're walkin' away," Jack reiterated.

Ray walked backwards for a few paces, then turned on his heel and scurried away as fast as he could.

I tried not to laugh (or puke) as I dropped my head to Jack's chest and breathed in his clean scent, wiping the Ray stench away. I wrapped my arms around him and sighed. "Thank you."

Jack slid his fingers into my hair, then stroked my back. "Missed you."

"You too," I whispered. "Are you ready?"

"Yeah. You gonna watch from the side?"

"Of course I am."

"I want to see you, baby."

I met his eyes and smiled. "I'll be there...well, unless, I'm puking. Then I'll be worshipping the porcelain god, or the nearest trash can."

"I thought this was going to be a dry tour. With all of this talk of you puking..."

"Since I'll probably be dry-heaving, you're not far off."

Jack laughed, kissing my temple.

"Oh!" I said. "I almost forgot, Bam asked us to watch their set tonight."

"Why's tonight special?"

"I don't know, but when my bestie asks me to do something easy, I try to accommodate."

Jack grinned and I slipped my hand in his as we walked to stage right. We stood in the wings, just behind the sightline of the heavy black curtain and watched Bam walk out from behind his kit, to stand center stage.

"We hope y'all are havin' a great time tonight!" Bam yelled.

The crowd roared back in appreciation.

Bam grinned. "We hear you, Boise, and we feel you, so we'd like to do something special for you tonight, if that's alright."

Another swell of applause.

Roses for Anna was on the rise, and as predicted, they were now playing to nearly full houses every night. They had previously headlined their own theater tour, so on the nights when they weren't opening for RatHound, I had them booked in smaller venues just to work each local market as much as possible. With their work ethic, talent, and the ever-growing reputation of their live shows, I saw no reason why Roses for Anna couldn't be the biggest rock band in America.

"We're gonna do a brand new song for you now, but we need a little help from someone really special to us. Please welcome my father-in-law, Rex Haddon!"

"What's this?" Jack asked.

I shrugged. "I honestly have no idea."

Bam continued, "We needed a fifth man to pull this job off so we called in a real pro. This is kind of different for us, so bear with us. This was written for some people that are very special to us. This is called Circle of Fear."

All four members of Roses for Anna, and Rex stood in a circle, in the center of the stage, and sang out, without accompaniment, in five-part harmony.

Within moments I was in tears. This was a love song written for me and Jack. I'd come to find out later that Bam and Rex had written the song in secret, and the band worked on it tirelessly until they had it perfect.

Rex broke away and sat down at the piano, and Edward picked up an acoustic guitar. They were joined by two string players during the song's final chorus, the entire song being led by this angelic five-piece choir of rough and tumble rock stars.

By the time they got to the chorus again, I was a sobbing, heaving wreck. Jack's t-shirt was soaked in my tears as I clung to him.

"I'm going to kill them. I'm going to murder them both.

It's not fair to play with a pregnant lady's emotions," I said through my tears.

The arena was as quiet as a church as they played. Quieter than any rock audience I've ever heard, but they erupted the moment the song ended. It was unlike anything I'd ever experienced.

When the song finished, Rex left the stage and came over for a hug.

I wrapped my arms around him and squeezed. "I can't believe you stupid jerks did that and that you were able to keep it from me. It was so beautiful, Rex. Great, now I'm crying again."

"It was all Bam's idea," he said, holding me tight. "You can blame him."

"Oh, believe you me, mister, I'll deal with him when he's done out there."

Rex smiled and he and Jack hugged. Rex walked back to Roxie, who practically dry-humped the man in front of everyone, and I slid into Jack's arms.

"You okay?" Jack asked.

"That was so beautiful."

"You're beautiful."

I wiped my still wet face. "I'm sure I look fabulous at the moment."

"Red carpet ready," he replied.

"Maybe as a stand-in for the carpet," I protested. "Puffy and bright red."

"Hadley, you don't get to talk about the mother of my child and my future bride like that." Jack pulled me in closer.

"You still want me to be your wife? Are you sure?"

"More sure than anything in my entire life."

"Everything has happened so fast, and life has been so crazy..."

"Life is always crazy. If I've learned anything, it's that

186

life is full of completely unexpected twists. Hadley, you have been the most unexpected twist of them all, and now we're going to have a baby. I couldn't be more sure of who you are and how I feel about you. I love you and I cannot imagine my life without you."

I thought I was crying before, but what was happening now was some next level shit.

CHAPTER
NINETEEN

Jack

THE BAND WAS on fire tonight. Rex, Robbie and I had never sounded or played better than we had on this tour. In fact, I'd happily pit our current selves against our younger selves in a rock-and-roll cage match. We'd chew those snotty punks up and spit 'em out. Unlike in the past, it felt to me like were now playing for bigger reasons than just to inflate our own egos or legend. We were no longer playing like kids with nothing to lose, but instead, like men that had *everything* to lose.

Each song in tonight's set seamlessly blended into the

next, and we pushed ourselves and each other harder and harder with each one. The crowd was so worked up, the room felt like it was going to burst by the time we neared the end of the show. Unfortunately, right about then, I became aware of something else about to burst.

The pain of playing drums with a blister is threefold. First there's the initial pain of the blister itself, not to mention having to alter your grip in order to accommodate it. Then there's the exciting jolt when it finally rips open midset, but neither of these compare to the final level of blister hell; the moment the stinging sweat of your hand finds its way to the raw, newly exposed flesh.

"Motherfucker!!!" I yelled out in pain as I came crashing down on my cymbals for the final note of the song. The stage lights darkened and Roger, my tech ran over with a flash light.

"What's up boss?"

"Fuckin' blister popped!" I hissed.

"I'll get you a bandage. Sit tight," he responded.

I knew I had a few minutes before my next cue and, as promised, Hadley had been at the side of the stage all night. I'm sure she was the reason I was playing with such intensity.

"Ask Hadley to grab the bottle of New Skin from my dressing case. She knows exactly where it is, and the code for the lock."

Roger did as he was asked and I waited as Rex began Song for Steven. This was one of our biggest hits, and to keep it from getting stale, we'd always changed it up a bit over the years. On this tour, Rex played and extended the piano intro while talking about the songs origins. Rex had lost his younger brother to suicide, but rarely talked about it in the past. These days it seemed like we were all opening up a lot more than we had back in the day.

My cue to enter was coming up, but there was no sign of

Roger or Hadley. I grabbed some gaffer's tape from my stick bag and field dressed my wound just as I would have back in our club days. The stage lights came up as Robbie and I began to play, and I could now see the sides of the stage clearly. There was no sign of Hadley, but I could see Roger hustling toward the stage.

He reached the monitoring desk and I heard his voice through my in-ears.

"Sorry boss, I couldn't find Hadley. I've got some bandages for ya whenever you're ready."

I gave him a nod and started scanning the stage again for Hadley.

She must have Anna business to tend to.

We finished our set, and as we took our bows, the crowd's energy swamped me, and I could really feel just how much we'd given tonight. Some nights on the road, you knew you'd given it your all, and this was one of those special nights.

"That's definitely the second most amount a fun a person is allowed to have!" Robbie yelled as we exited the stage.

"If you're looking for arguments, you'll fine none from me brother," Rex replied. "You were pounding the shit outta those things, Jack. You were almost louder than Robbie on stage."

"What can I say, I'm...inspired," I said.

"Fucking possessed is more like it," Robbie said, smiling.

I was smiling on the outside, but starting to feel uneasy.

Where the fuck is Hadley?

I scanned our entourage as we walked through the arena halls, toward our dressing room. No Hadley, but I saw Ray walking alongside Bam, so at least I knew that little cheese dick didn't have her pinned in some dark corner somewhere.

"Has anyone seen Hadley?" I asked to our group, but got nothing in return.

As we approached the dressing room, I quickened my pace. I passed the others, then security and swung the door to our suite open.

No sign of her.

"Hadley!" I called out.

Rex and Roxie were right behind me, followed by our ever-increasing train of people.

"What's wrong, Jack? I'm sure she's just tied up with business somewhere," Rex said.

"No. Something's wrong. She was supposed to have her eyes locked on mine all night. She promised. Hadley doesn't break promises."

Bam pushed through the crowd and yelled out "Hadley!"

The dressing suite had three smaller rooms off the large main area we were currently standing in. Bam stood closest to the far-left dressing room door, and swung it wide open to reveal an empty room. I opened the door to the far right and my blood ran cold.

"Don't move or I'll cut her."

Cathy Meadows was on the floor with her back against the far wall of the dressing room. Her legs were spread wide and she had Hadley in front of her, with a butcher knife to her throat. There was blood smeared on the wall behind them, and blood all over both Cathy and Hadley.

I held my hand out. "Cathy, I—"

"Don't say a word and don't come any closer or I swear I will make you a widower a second time." Cathy's voice was flat and soulless. "I know she's not your wife yet, which I guess would make this even more tragic."

I saw Hadley tremble and her eyes widen. Cathy's left hand was covering her mouth, securing her head tightly in place. She held the knife tightly to Hadley's throat, and she was significantly larger than Hadley, giving her complete control.

I stood perfectly still.

"Oh, good. You *do* have the ability to stay still and listen to someone," Cathy said. "Don't worry. We won't be interrupted by any emergency phone calls this time."

I raised my hands and bowed my head slightly in an effort to show contrition. Cathy held the knife closer, causing Hadley to bleed. I wanted to lunge at Cathy and kill her with my bare hands, but couldn't risk pushing her over the edge any further.

"Don't you dare say you're sorry," Cathy continued. "Thanks for that little charade by the way. That little phone call ended up being hotel security, who detained me, packed up my belongings, and escorted me into a taxi. Now, why would they do that I wonder? Maybe it's because some stuck-up bitch newcomer that doesn't know her place in this band, called security on me and made up a bunch of lies about me because she's jealous!"

Cathy peered past me, craning her neck to see the crowd behind me.

"Who's out there?" she asked. "Move out of the way so I can see. Slowly!"

I did as she asked, my eyes locked on Hadley's.

"Is Rex Haddon out there?" Cathy called out.

"I'm here," Rex replied calmly.

"You come in here, Rex, it's okay," she said, the tone of her voice showing the first sign of humanity, then sharply added, "and if anyone calls security, this bitch is dead before they reach the door."

"No one is calling security," I said.

"I thought I told you to shut your fucking mouth, *Jack*."

The way she said my name let me know exactly how detached from reality this woman was. I still couldn't tell where all the blood was coming from, but Hadley's shirt was soaked.

"Hi, Rex." Cathy broke into a creepy smile the moment Rex entered the room, but her body remained tightly wound around Hadley.

"Hello," Rex said, cautiously avoiding eye contact.

"It's okay, silly, it's me...Cathy. Come in so we can talk."

Rex's eyes met mine and I could tell he was in the fucking dark.

"Okay, let's talk...Cathy is it?"

"Come on, Rex, don't act like you don't recognize me," she said. "It's only been a couple of years since the last time we met face-to-face...plus all the emails, most of which have gone unanswered lately."

"I'm sorry, Cathy, I meet a lot of people, so sometimes my memory isn't so great, but I do think I remember meeting you—"

Cathy stopped smiling.

"You *think* you remember me? I'm the whole reason you're even here tonight Rex. It's bad enough you didn't even bother to send me free tickets. I thought maybe you were waiting to surprise me with backstage passes to the last show of the tour or something, but you didn't even do that. Then rock star Jack Henry big times me, and I'm the whole reason he's back in the band."

"I'm sorry, Cathy, I'm not sure I follow. Maybe I'm just not thinking straight because of the knife on my very good friend there."

"Your friend? You mean this whore that does your dirty work? This bitch right here that has your most loyal fans thrown out of hotel rooms? Like the fan that gave you the idea to get Jack Henry and Robbie back together to re-form RatHound?"

Cathy was panting, squeezing Hadley tighter, and my

stomach roiled worse and worse with each second.

"You're right," Rex said carefully. "I remember now that it *was* you that said we should get the band back together, and I apologize for not returning your emails. All email goes through our PR firm, but it looks like there was a mistake, because I must have not gotten yours. I will rectify that immediately so we make sure you get the credit you deserve."

I saw Cathy's eyes start to soften.

"It's just a little confusing to me as to why you'd let Jack treat me this way, when you told me yourself how vitally important I am to this band." Cathy started to tear up.

"You are important Cathy," Rex said.

"I know, because when we first met at your solo show in Tampa in 2010, and I was wearing my favorite RatHound shirt, and you told me that I was vitally important to the band's legacy, and that's when I knew you understood me, and that I understand your message even when no one else heard it." Her rambling was become more and more intense.

"That's right," Rex said reassuringly. "And I know that Jack and Hadley didn't mean to hurt your feelings. That's my fault, Cathy. I didn't tell them who you are, and I should have, and I apologize from the bottom of my heart. I'd hate for Hadley to get hurt because of my stupid mistake."

"If I'd have known how important you were..." I said, and cringed when Hadley whimpered as Cathy shifted the knife. "What if you and I start over from scratch? We could spend some time talking in the dressing room, just the two of us, alone."

"You think I'm gonna believe a word that comes out of your mouth? You broke up this band once before over a woman, and now you're letting this whore chase off the people that are vitally important to this band." Cathy rose to her feet, Hadley still at the mercy of her blade. "Vitally important, Jack. I'm the lifeblood of RatHound. I understand the message that Rex is trying to send to his true listeners and that you and Robbie are his instruments. You've strayed, and allowed this whore—"

Hadley gave one powerful thrust to Cathy's solar plexus and then dropped to her knees.

A loud boom echoed in the room, and Cathy's head snapped back before her body hit the floor. Before she could recover, I rushed in between them, divesting Cathy of the knife and sliding it across the room.

Sully called out, "All clear!" and I turned to see him armed with a shotgun.

"Is she dead?" I asked.

"Just knocked out. She took a bean bag round to the forehead."

I helped Hadley to her feet and she immediately began kicking Cathy's still unconscious body.

"That's right, bitch! Call me a whore one more time!"

I could now see the blood everywhere was definitely not Cathy's.

"Where the fuck's all that blood coming from?" I snapped.

"My hand," Hadley rasped.

"Did she cut you anywhere else?" I asked.

Hadley shook her head. "Just my hand, when I was trying to fight her off."

"My guys are taking care of the woman," Sully said. "I'll drive you to the hospital. It'll be faster than calling an ambulance."

I nodded and scooped Hadley into my arms as gently as I could.

"Honey, my legs aren't broken."

"Not takin' any chances in you passin' out," I said,

maybe a little curter than I should have, but I was trying not to completely lose my shit.

We followed Sully out to the car and I set her inside, then I climbed in beside her and secured her seatbelt. Sully started the car and took off and I focused on Hadley and her breathing. I'd never driven with Lucy's bodyguard, but he drove a car like he was one with it, delivering us to the hospital in less than five minutes. I helped Hadley out of the car and wrapped an arm firmly around her waist as we rushed inside. "I need help!" I bellowed.

"How can I help?" the receptionist asked.

"My wife, she's losing blood."

"Right, sir, we just need you to fill out—"

"Fuck the paperwork! Get someone out here to take care of her."

Sully stepped between me and the desk, leaning over to speak quietly to the woman. Within seconds, a nurse arrived with a wheelchair and I lifted Hadley into it. Her color did not look good, and I was concerned she might pass out.

"She's pregnant," I said.

"We'll take care of her," the nurse assured me, and we headed into the back.

In the end, it took twelve stitches to close the wound on her hand. Hadley had fought for the knife and obviously held on a little longer than she should have, because Cathy had a better grip and ripped it away, slicing Hadley's palm in the process.

The baby was fine, and other than the cut and a few bruises, Hadley was too. She was allowed to leave a few hours after we arrived, so Sully drove us back to the hotel. I helped her get rid of her bloody clothes and shower, then settled her into bed with an order to stay there until the following afternoon.

"I'm fine, honey," she argued.

"I'm aware." I smiled. "But, regardless, you're stayin'
in this bed 'til I feel better."

She wrinkled her nose. "Bossy—"

"Yeah, I'm aware." I leaned down to kiss her. "Ain't
gonna change anything."

She flopped back on the pillows. "Killjoy."

I sat on the edge of the mattress. "How's your pain level?"

"It's fine."

I stroked her cheek. "You bein' a hero?"

She smiled...fuckin' finally. "No. I'm good, honey.
Promise."

"You wanna talk about it?"

She shook her head, her hair falling in front of her face.
"Not yet."

"I'm here."

It took a minute, but she met my eyes. "I know."

"Love you, baby."

"Love you too." She kissed me gently. "Can I curl up on
the sofa and watch a movie if I promise not to move from
there? We can snuggle. I don't want to be in this bed all
night."

I sighed. "I'll allow it."

She chuckled. "Thank you, oh benevolent one."

I helped her to the sofa and grabbed the comforter from
the bed laying it over her. As I snagged a pillow to set behind her, a knock at the door came. I opened it to find Sully.
"Hey, man."

"Mr. Henry." He nodded. "I just wanted to check on
Hadley."

"Come in." I stepped back and Sully made his way to
Hadley.

"It's the Sullynator," she joked.

He chuckled. "You doing okay, Miss Simon?"

"I'm doing great. You, Jack and Rex are my heroes,"

she said. "What happened with the crazy lady?"

"She's with the authorities. I've reached out to some contacts and she won't be a problem again."

"Thank you," she whispered.

"I'm going to let you rest now, but I'll be driving you and Mr. Henry home tomorrow."

"What about Lucy?"

"She requested I stay with you."

Hadley met my eyes and I nodded. I'd approved Sully's guard for the next couple of days, but I liked that she wanted to make sure I was okay with it.

"Thanks, Sully," she said.

"My pleasure, Miss Simon." He grinned. "I'll be back."

Hadley giggled, and fuck me, I loved that sound.

Sully left the room and I settled in for a quiet night with my girl...even if we did have to watch the Notebook.

Hadley

W E WERE HOME.

Well, we were at Rex and Roxie's guest house and I was trying to unpack, but my hand hurt like a mofo. The drugs the doctor gave me helped...sort of. At least enough so I could sleep, but unpacking was tough to do one-handed.

I also couldn't play drums and I had been dying to play Jack's kit during the entire tour. We were either trying to keep a low profile, broken up, or dodging sleazy promoters and homicidal maniacs, so could never quite make that happen.

Tonight was the last night of the tour, and now it looked like I'd miss my chance once again.

"Baby, I'll do that," Jack said, wrapping an arm around my waist and tugging me away from my bag.

I sighed, facing him and dropping my head to his chest. "I think I'm going to have to let you."

"Why is your lip sticking out like that?"

"I'm pouting."

He stroked my back. "And why are you pouting?"

"Because I want to play your drums at sound check and I can't."

"I'm sorry, baby. There will be other tours I'm sure."

"Really?"

"A few small conversations have taken place. We'll see what happens."

She sighed. "I love the idea of being on the road with you again."

"What about Roses for Anna?"

"I'll just need to book their tours on different dates than yours."

I chuckled. "I like where your head's at."

She kissed me gently. "Can't wait to watch you tonight."

"We should probably head out, huh?"

"Yes, but you have to promise me you'll take care of me after the show...no assing out from final night adrenaline fall."

"When have I ever assed out of taking care of you."

She grinned. "This is the correct answer, fiancé."

I laughed and helped her with her hair so we could head to the venue.

* * *

I'd always hated the last night of the tour. Mostly because I hated goodbyes, but also because for some reason, I was afraid that if I got off the road, I'd never be able to get back on. For these reasons, I had spent my entire adult life in motion; moving from one adventure to the next.

Tonight was different. My next adventure revolved around Hadley and our child, and I wouldn't even have to leave home to experience that.

"Are you ready?" Hadley asked squeezing my hand.

"For tonight? Yes. For every day after that...?"

She smiled and we entered the final venue of the tour together. We were ending in our hometown of Seattle, and after the great reviews throughout the tours, the critical and public success of the new EP and the added tabloid notoriety of the "crazy stalker lady," we were the absolute talk of the town.

After we'd finished sound check and Hadley was done with her usual administration work, I texted her meet me near the stage. I wouldn't tell her why and I was quickly learning that surprises drove her crazy.

"What is it?" she begged for information as I blindfolded her and led her up the side stairs.

"Would you just trust me?" I said.

I walked her over to the drum riser, sat her down at my throne, and removed her blindfold.

She squealed in delight, but then stopped. Looking down at her hand she said, "But what about my hand?"

Just as the words left her mouth, I cued our sound man, and Pour Some Sugar on Me came pumping through the massive sound system.

"They're playing our song, baby, and Rick Allen only needed one arm, so go for it!"

I watched as Hadley literally single handedly rocked the fuck out with everything she had. It was glorious and I couldn't have loved her more at that moment.

As I watched her play (amazingly well, despite her injury), I glanced over at Rex who was also enjoying the show. I gave him a nod, then focused back on Hadley. My future wife, my now family, and I wondered at all I'd been given in such a short amount of time.

I'd traveled a dark, dark path, but Hadley Simon had shown me the road back.

Hadley

Three years later...

"**P**USH, BABY!" JACK encouraged. "You can do it."

I was currently giving birth to our second child and I honestly wanted to smack my husband upside the head. He'd been the consummate cheerleader, but right now, I just wanted him to stick his hands inside my body and pull the baby moose out. "She's too big."

"You're doing great, Hadley," Doctor Milstad said. "I

see the head."

Another four pushes and our little girl came into the world screaming like the future rock star she was destined to be. I'd been in labor for over twenty hours, and I was pretty wiped out, but the face of my big, strong husband sobbing at the sight of our baby as the nurse settled her in my arms was worth it all.

"Hi, there, sweet pea. Happy birthday." I kissed her little forehead. "I'm your Mama, and right there is the daddy who's already bought a couple of guns for when the boys come around."

Jack chuckled, leaning down to kiss her. "Three guns. I bought three."

Ryan Pamela Gornitzka looked up at her daddy and blinked.

"You have a big brother waiting to meet you," I continued.

Samuel Rex was two-years-old, the greatest kid on the planet, and a pretty damn good drummer, which wasn't a surprise, considering who his father was. Uncle Rex and Roxie were spoiling him rotten while we were welcoming his baby sister into the world.

"I love you," Jack whispered, kissing us both. "You've given me everything, baby."

I stroked his cheek. "Right there with you, honey."

Ryan wrapped her fingers around one of his and Jack grinned. "She's perfect."

"Yes, she is."

We spent the next two hours ogling our daughter before Roxie walked in with Sammy and then it was all about him snuggling the new baby, which was the cutest damn thing on the planet.

As our family filed in deto visit, I thought about the whirlwind our life had been over the last three years. We'd been married a week after the final show in Seattle at Rex

204

and Roxie's home, then Jack took me back to Mobile to pack up my apartment and give notice. We'd lived at the guest house for six months while we looked for a house, nothing seemed right, so we ended up building not far from Rex and Roxie. Samuel had arrived early, so even though the house was done on time, Jack refused to move in until I was up to it. This suited me fine, because it meant I could order furniture and we moved in as soon as it arrived.

Lucy and I had swapped positions. She was now managing Roses for Anna and I was managing RatHound. It made more sense, especially considering Bam and Lucy moved to Alabama. Rex lost his mind for a few weeks, but once Samuel arrived, we made sure Rex was distracted by the new addition to the family, and Samuel was able to sooth Rex's ache of missing Lucy.

A summer tour was planned to start in six months, so with two babies and a band to manage, my life was hectic…deliciously so. Roses for Anna would be double-billing for a few dates, so it would be an incredible family reunion.

When Bam and Lucy walked into the hospital room, I burst into tears and hugged them. "What are you guys doing here?"

Lucy grinned, kissing Ryan. "Sully flew us in as soon as Mom called to say you were in labor. We couldn't miss the birth of our niece."

I nodded to her expanding belly. "Are you allowed to fly?"

She chuckled. "Stop it, Beau junior. I have three months left, it's perfectly safe."

I marveled at the family I'd been blessed with. We might not all be related, but I loved them more than I could love anyone, and as my husband showed off his children proudly, I beamed at the beautiful man before me.

I was loved, I was honored, and I was the luckiest woman alive.

ABOUT JACK & PIPER

Piper Davenport writes from a place of passion and intrigue, combining elements of romance and suspense with strong modern day heroes and heroines.

She currently resides in pseudonymia under the dutiful watch of the Writers Protection Agency.

Like Piper's FB page and get to know her!
(www.facebook.com/piperdavenport)
Twitter: @piper_davenport
Sign up for her mailing list!

Jack Davenport is a true romantic at heart, but he has a rebel's soul. His writing is passionate, energetic, and often fueled by his true life, fiery romance with author wife, Piper Davenport. A musician by day, his unique perspective into the world of rock stars provides an exciting backdrop for his new romance series.

He currently lives with his wife and two kids in the top left corner of the United States.

Like Jack's FB page and get to know him!
(www.facebook.com/jackdavenportauthor)

Made in the USA
Coppell, TX
27 January 2021

48875566R00125